SWORDS OF E

BOOK ONE OF THE SHAMA

Robert Ryan

Cover design by www.damonza.com

ISBN: 9798835954391
(print edition)

Trotting Fox Press

Contents

Prologue

Halls of Lore: Chamber 8. Aisle 64. Item 16
General subject: Fall of the Cheng Empire
Topic: The assassination of Chen Fei
Author: An historical treatise translated by Malach Gan

The land wept blood, and the cries of the innocent lifted into the heavens. Yet no answer came save for the drum of iron-shod boots marching to battle and the clash of sword on shield.

So it was in the long years after the Shadowed Wars that saw the fall of dark gods and the rise of heroes. Yet the legends of those days speak seldom of hunger, poverty and the wailing of mothers whose children were beaten down in war and left unburied, their bones bleached beneath the hammering sun.

Warbands preyed on the weak, and the strong built fortresses. The kings who once ruled the lands of the Cheng had fallen in the Shadowed Wars, and those who sought inheritance of their power squabbled among each other like dogs contesting a carcass.

Kingdoms became divided clans, and chiefs ruled their small tribes with savage hearts and lust for the glory that had been lost. The great wars of Light against Dark were replaced by petty skirmishes. Swift raids to steal cattle, sheep and women were common, and each clan despised their neighbors. Mistrust and hatred ruled, and the laws the old kings had made in the name of justice were

Third was the might of all the shamans combined. They came at him in the midnight hour, their spirits from all over the land joined to form a single shadow-man that fought with two swords as did he. Chen Fei was wounded near to death, yet still he broke the spell with his blades and many shamans who could not swiftly separate from their creation perished with it. Their servants found them dead in their tents the next morning, slashed by swords though they had been alone.

The shamans withdrew then to their stronghold in Three Moon Mountain, and they were seen no more for seven years. Yet their plotting did not end.

In those years, the last of the chiefdoms fell under Chen Fei's sway and he ruled all the lands of the Cheng. An emperor he became, and the citizens thrived.

Chen Fei was the greatest leader in the history of his people. His friends loved him. His enemies feared him. Among the populace his very name became a byword for peace and terror both, for even as he wielded two swords so too there were twin aspects to his nature. Yet to do good a leader must be strong against his enemies.

After their time of self-imposed exile, the shamans returned to the land. They pretended fealty to Chen Fei, but he mistrusted them. All the while they sought to destabilize the empire and secretly incite rebellion, stirring up old rivalries between clans and promoting discord.

The emperor made war against them, and after seven years of retreat, mistrusted by most and shunned by many, they fled once more to their mountain, and the people said it was angry for thunder rumbled from it during the day and strange lights flashed skyward at night.

The nation prospered, and Chen Fei at last knew peace. He had fathered many children, and they themselves became parents. During this time, Olekhai, the chief of his council of wise men, became a close friend. And seven more years passed wherein the land waxed fairly.

But even as the hidden worm gnaws inside the apple, there was darkness amid the light, for Olekhai betrayed his friend. The shamans bought his heart, and with gold and jewels and promises of the emperor's throne they lured him into treachery.

It was done with swift poison, for even in age none dared fight Chen Fei sword to sword. And as he lay dying, the betrayer let into the room three shamans, and they mocked their enemy.

Chen Fei bestirred himself, and wracked with pain and half blind he rose from the floor and they retreated from him in fear. Yet he could not follow, so he spoke.

"Hear me, accursed shamans. Think ye the victory is thine? It is not so. One day, though the time be distant, of my blood a new ruler will rise, and they will purge your order from the world. Ye shall know that day is come when they wield my swords, and when ye look into eyes like mine again. Then fear will unman ye, and your evil deeds will tramp up from behind and overtake ye at the last."

And Chen Fei died. The shamans seized his swords, using the dead emperor's own hands to place them in a wooden box, for they had learned of the magic in them. They fled in haste, yet they deserted Olekhai and left him to the wrath of Shulu Gan who returned to the city after an errand.

Shulu Gan wept for the emperor, and for all that was lost and for all that would yet come. Even as grief overtook her, the shamans set in motion the worst of their dark plot, and it is not said their followers stinted at the bloody deeds. The relatives of the emperor were assassinated. Poison killed some. Others fell to the flash of hidden blades. Men, women, children and babes all died. The shamans would not suffer one of Chen Fei's offspring to assume his throne.

Shulu Gan dried her tears, and she had Olekhai brought to her in his chains, for he had been caught trying to flee the palace. Nigh to death that man came, and it would have been a mercy to give it to him. Yet the wrath of Shulu Gan was very great, and it was cold also, more pitiless in that hour than the deeps of the void.

"I shall not kill you," she told him, and her voice was like the whisper of a knife in its sheath. "Rather shall I give you life everlasting. Yet no man in the land will succor you. No man will be able to kill you. Nor will you be able to take your own life, though you will weary of it as a burden that cannot be borne. That which you eat will taste of ashes, and that which you drink will be as dust. Yet treachery will eat your heart, and neither peace nor comfort will you ever know."

"Mercy!" begged the man, but Shulu Gan had little. She placed her hands about the man's head, and though there was no sign of sorcery Olekhai staggered back and screamed.

"Unchain him," Shulu Gan commanded, and it was done. "Flee, you fool," she said. "Regret for your wickedness will rend your soul until an emperor once more sits upon the throne."

The years marched forward, and there was no new emperor nor would be. The shamans had come forth from Three Moon Mountain and seeded war and chaos across the land, all the while pretending to quell it. The empire fell, as they wished, and chiefdoms rose again. The shamans held great authority in each, and though the lands were divided they ruled as one even as a spider that spins many connected webs.

Yet the words of the dying emperor troubled them, and more so his twin swords, for they tried to destroy them by all their arts and could not. The skill of Shulu Gan surpassed their lore, and they sought her to discover the secrets of their forging, but she was gone, though they knew she was not dead. So at last they hid the blades and guarded them, and they killed all babes born with pale eyes to forestall the emperor's prophecy.

The toll in blood of their cruelty was high, for though the Cheng were a dark-eyed people yet still blue eyes were seen, though violet was rarer. But as the years grew old they found fewer and fewer, and at length none. Then the prophecy of the emperor slept.

But it was not forgotten. And a legend grew that Shulu Gan had saved one child of the emperor's blood, and that she plotted her revenge…

1. Twisted Trails

Shar smelled the night wind, and there was smoke on it. It was not the scent of a homely campfire, but rather a token of destruction.

She wished to help, for there were those out there, not far away, who needed it. If they were still alive. But duty held her back, for she was under orders.

It occurred to her to disobey. She had little fear of reprimand, for in the face of tragedy a reprimand was nothing. Yet her orders, though they chafed her at the moment, were for the good of the whole clan. The Fen Wolves relied on her now, though they did not know it yet. The information she had been sent to obtain was important, and if she failed in her mission then others might die that need not.

So she climbed a little higher into the dense crown of the tree that was her hiding place, and waited for the dawn.

Already the eastern sky was pale, and the gray fingers of the new day touched everything, giving a promise of what was to come.

The scent of smoke and ash was still strong, though it was beginning to fade and the usual swamp smells of stagnant water and decaying vegetation came to her strongly. Travelers never liked it, but to her it was home. It was earthy. It spoke to her of all her childhood that was gone, and of learning the ways of Tsarin Fen that were mysterious, dangerous and yet magical.

The sun rose slowly above the rim of the world. It was a ball of red fire for the smoke in the air colored it so, and its light began to show what she knew was there yet did not want to see.

A village lay outside the perimeter of the swamp. The inhabitants were still Fen Wolves, but they had taken to the flat grasslands at some time in the distant past. The grass was better for the pasturing of animals, and there was less sickness among the stock, yet that benefit came at increased risk.

The village was in the open, and it was closer to the enemies of the clan. The Soaring Eagle Tribe dwelt out here, and they did not like their lands encroached upon. In the past, their attacks had been fended off, but this time they must have come in larger numbers.

Gritting her teeth, Shar gazed at the village. It lay in ruins, and smoke drifted lazily up from it. Every hut had been destroyed, and though she could not see the corpses she knew they were there. Already the crows were at work, and she saw clusters of them in many places, and even over the mile or so of open space she could hear their squawking as they feasted.

The flocks of sheep that the villagers raised had been herded together. Even as Shar watched she saw men begin to drive them southward toward the heartland of the Soaring Eagles. Yet those men were few.

Concerningly, the majority were camped a little way to the west. It was a large raiding party, perhaps thirty strong as far as she could see, but it was hard to tell for they were preparing to march themselves and their moving to and fro as they broke camp made it hard to gauge their true number.

Yet why had they not gone with the shepherds?

Shar watched, and her every muscle was tense. She let out a slow breath and calmed herself. The villagers were beyond her help now, and all that she could do was to report back to her superiors what had occurred. They

13

would make the necessary decisions, and for that they relied on accurate information.

The warriors showed little sign of anxiousness. They were close to Fen Wolf lands, even arguably upon them, but they had only one man set as sentry watching the swamp for sign of retaliation. Either they were complacent, or they knew the size of the patrols that regularly scouted the borderlands, and knew they outnumbered them.

Shar had a dark suspicion as to which of those it was. Her patrol was only half the size of the enemy. Not only that, they were timid too. The patrol leader was a good man, but his orders from the chief were to patrol only and avoid any conflict, if possible. They were good orders, so far as they went, but they did not account for enemy aggression such as this. So it was that she had been sent alone to gather information last night when they first smelled the smoke. The whole patrol would more likely be detected if they went, but one scout, especially the best, which Shar was, could discover what was happening and report back without being seen.

She nearly descended the tree, wishing to travel the mile back into the swamp and tell her leader what she had seen, but she waited instead.

And it was well that she did. Unbelievably, when the enemy began to march they did not follow the shepherds back into Soaring Eagle territory. Instead, they struck forward, toward the fen, and toward her also.

Again she considered descending the tree, but there was a chance she might be seen as she came out of the canopy, but also staying where she was would give her the best view.

The day grew brighter. There was a plop as some lizard or other animal submerged itself in water nearby, and from the distance came the repeated cry of a moorhen, the sound of the fens themselves.

The enemy came on, and they drew close to the edge of the wetlands and there paused, hesitant to proceed forward. Foreigners had a fear for the swamp, and not without cause. It was dangerous for the unwary to travel, and getting lost in the thick growth or sunk in hidden mud were not the only threats. But after a careful look, they commenced marching again, if slower, and angled exactly toward where Shar was hidden.

She remained still and watched. Raids had increased lately, but this was the first time in her life that the Soaring Eagles had ventured past the easy targets of fringe settlements and into the wetlands themselves.

Yet the patrols of the Fen Wolves could not be everywhere. The *leng-fah*, and she thought of that name with pride for it meant wolf skills, and the fen wolf was the revered totem of her tribe, were great scouts and warriors, but they could not discover and protect against all attacks. Yet still, the move of the enemy was bold.

The warriors passed below her very tree, and she held herself still and watched. They were tall men, taller than Fen Wolves for the most part, and the eagle feather each wore in their headband made them seem taller still.

There was little noise from their movement, for they went slowly. They were not skilled in the swamp though, for any Fen Wolf child could move at many times that pace and make still less sound.

At length, with many a backward glance, and frequent wary looks to the undergrowth at their sides, they disappeared from sight. For all their caution though, they had not looked upward into the tree.

Shar waited. Time was pressing, for she must return to the leng-fah and bring warning of what was happening, yet she could not risk that a straggler might see her, or still worse a rear guard might be deliberately scouring their backtrail for signs of scouts.

She let the minutes pass by, calmly watching, and when she felt secure she deftly came down out of the canopy and half climbed, half slid, down the trunk.

Wasting no time she set off down the same trail as the Soaring Eagles. Her eyes were itchy, as they often were. It was a small thing though. Otherwise, she felt strong and healthy, and nearby were those who were dead.

She thought swiftly as she walked. This was more than a raid. Something else was going on, and she must discover what. But all her choices carried risks. She could just report back to her leader, but the enemy was between her and the leng-fah. She had a plan for that when she drew closer, but she could only report what the enemy had done that way, not what their intention was. To find out what that was, something bolder was needed.

It was not long before she came up close to them. She heard them edging forward, even slower now than they had been. They did not speak much, though here and there she heard a soft voice or a grunt at some misstep into mud as they navigated the twisted trails of the fen.

Then her opportunity came. Trailing behind them was one of their scouts. She saw him, though he did not see her. He was watching their backtrail carefully, and fear was graven into his face. He did not like being alone, even if he was still within call of his companions.

Shar eased a little to the left, and then she sped up. She could see the scout no more, but as she drew level with him she could hear his faint footfalls, and she veered right again, using a stunted stand of hoary oaks as cover. Now, she heard his very breath, and she waited in silence.

The man stepped near the tree behind which she stood, and he turned his head back to study the empty swamp behind him. He did not even sense her as she slipped from hiding, tripped him and flung him to the ground with a hand over his mouth to stifle any yell and a knife at his throat.

"Make one sound," she hissed softly, "and this knife will slice your neck open." She pressed the cold metal against his skin to reinforce her words.

She looked into his eyes, and she saw wild fear there. Her own were cold and determined.

"If you do as you're told, I promise you'll live. If you try to warn your friends, you *will* die. Do you understand?"

The man nodded slowly, careful of the blade at his neck.

Shar waited then. Already she had risked much by talking to him softly, but soon the Soaring Eagle warriors passed beyond earshot, unless it was a yell. So she spoke again, and this time she took her hand from the man's mouth.

"Answer quietly and truthfully," she commanded him. "Where is the warband going?"

She could see in his eyes that he had thought of yelling out, but he knew the knife would kill him before he could have taken a deep breath for it.

"Deep into the fen," he answered.

"Not good enough," Shar hissed. "Where and why?"

"I don't know where, exactly. That I swear. Only our leader does. But at the command of our shaman we're to strike hard into the fen and destroy at least several villages before returning."

Something in his words rang hollow to Shar. "Your band is too small for that. The villages inside the fen are mostly larger than the one you just raided. Tell me the truth, or die."

Even under that threat, and with the knife pressed hard at his throat, the warrior remembered his courage. She could see him think, but at last he succumbed as any would who cherished life.

"They go to meet a second band of warriors, coming in from farther to the east. There's a prearranged meeting point we should reach before dusk, but I don't know exactly where."

Shar felt a cold shiver run up her spine. This was more than a raid. It was a test of defenses such as might be done when war was contemplated. At any rate, she had learned what was needed.

In truth, she should kill the man. But she had given her word, and there was another means to subdue him for long enough that he could not go after his companions and give warning. Deftly, she gripped his arm and sunk one of her fingertips deep into the flesh, finding the pressure point that she sought and applying force at the angle she had been taught. Simultaneously, she released the knife and found the other point she wanted in the man's neck. He stiffened and trembled, then his head lolled to the side and he was unconscious.

He would stay so for a good while, and there would likely be no lasting ill effects. But the practice of *dar shun*, pressure point striking, was dangerous. There was some risk to him, but she was glad to have had the knowledge to save his life. Otherwise she must have used the knife.

Quickly she looked through his things, taking note of his weapons and how well forged they were. Likewise, she studied his rations, for the amount of them would tell her how long the warband intended to stay in the fen, or how deep they wished to penetrate. This at least gave her some relief, for there was only enough for a few days.

She gathered his weapons, which included several knives, and flung them away into thick growth nearby. This would slow him down more when he woke. Then she stood, and gazed in the direction the warriors had taken. They were between her and her companions, and they threatened her homeland. What was she to do?

2. The Call of the Wolf

Shar hastened forward, and she felt a weight of responsibility on her shoulders.

Yet she had trained for this as all the leng-fah had. They were the first line of defense against intrusions, and they had the skills of scouts and warriors both.

The enemy had continued along their path in as straight a line as the fen allowed, and where they had veered aside to avoid boggy ground and patches of open water, she had no trouble following their trail. Of greater risk was the chance that they had discovered their rear scout was no longer there, and that they had set a trap for her.

There was nothing out of place though, that she could see. So she hastened forward, even if with great caution. Soon she heard signs of the Soaring Eagles ahead, and then she paused. It was enough to locate them for now. For what she did next it was better not to be too close.

She waited, melding into the shadow of one of those hoary oaks that dominated the dryer lands of the fen. She was still, but her gaze covered all the landscape nearby, seeking signs of an enemy scout. She saw none, nor did she hear any.

Time passed swiftly, and she knew she could not wait too long. The enemy were heading toward where her companions were camped, and at all costs she must warn them before they were discovered and a battle broke out.

Taking a deep breath and cupping her hands to her mouth, she gave the wild, haunting howl of a fen wolf. This she had practiced for many years until only a fen-dweller could tell if it was animal or human, and even then but rarely. She was not the best in her patrol at it, but she was still skilled, and as always voicing the cry of her totem animal made the hair on the back of her neck rise.

She paused, allowing a deep silence to fall over the fen. Her patrol would hear that, and understand the signal in it. *Fall back. An enemy is near.*

Once more she cupped her hands to her mouth and voiced the call of the wolf. It would sound the same as the first to the enemy, yet to a member of the Fen Wolf Tribe the slight variation in notes said something different. *Go west. One mile.*

She did not linger after that. The enemy must sooner or later discover that their rear scout was gone. They would not know if he had fallen foul of her tribe or succumbed to some danger of the swamp, of which there were many, but they might halt and send out searchers for him. It was best that she was gone.

There was little chance any of her tracks would be discovered. She trod carefully, and she had followed in the trail the enemy themselves had made. They would not distinguish any sign she left from their own.

The sun was well up, and it was turning into a warm spring day. She hastened westward, and gauged the distance she traveled carefully. It was easy to move less distance than one thought they had, for the swamp made half a mile feel like two miles of travel in the open. When she approached the place where she thought her patrol would be, she would give another call and wait for an answer. More likely she would find them without that.

They had not answered her earlier wolf call, but that did not concern her. She knew they were close enough to hear, and it was considered better not to reply. Should an enemy discern the calls were of people rather than animals, it would also tell them where those people were.

Even so, she felt suddenly alone and vulnerable. For all her training, she had not been in a situation like this before. She wanted to feel the presence of the leng-fah about her. They were the closest thing to a family she had, saving only her grandmother. And her grandmother was not really related to her either.

The trail she followed, if trail it could be called for few beside a Fen Wolf would even see it, began to slope downward. The flies grew bothersome, constantly irritating her, but the mosquitoes were worse.

Ahead lay a body of water. She knew it well, and knew also that dangerous creatures lived there. They were larger than most in the fen, for the water here was deeper than in many places and able to conceal their bulk. It did not deter her, but she slowed a little and moved even more cautiously.

There was a noise overhead, though she could not see it because of the tree canopy. It startled her for a moment, but soon she identified what it was. She knew all the sounds of the swamp, and anything she heard that she did not know was likely an intruder of some sort and dangerous. But this was a snipe, a *ghirlock* as her grandmother called it though others in the clan never used that name. It meant the goat that flies, for it sounded like a goat and the legend was that the sound was the noise of a god in a goat-pulled cart traversing the sky. She did not believe that, yet the gods themselves were real. Of that, she was sure.

She grinned. The fen was full of creatures and sounds like that. They were eerie and unnerving, unless one knew what they were. The Soaring Eagle warriors must have heard many strange things such as this by now, and it would fuel fear and suspicion in them. That was to their disadvantage, for a nervous warrior fought a thousand battles and tired themselves before the real one confronted them.

She pushed ahead, and the body of water came into view on her left. Some might call it a lake, but she did not. Though it seemed deep water, there were many places where the earth was near the surface, and these were treacherous for the ground was not solid. Yet there were also deep stretches, and in some of these the creatures of the swamp dwelt.

A mosquito stung the side of her neck, and she brushed it away only to see another that she had not felt on the back of her hand. All this was part of the swamp, and she was used to it, but she did not like it.

Across the murky water, covered in pond scum that made the deep and shallow tracts all look alike, something moved. She was not sure what, but it was always best to assume the worst. It was said the creatures that lived in places such as this left people alone, for the most part. But it was also said that if driven by hunger they might come up onto dry land in pursuit of prey.

There was nothing out there now, save a slow ripple that lifted the pond scum a little before it settled back into place again. Perhaps it had merely been a fish. Or perhaps not.

Shar drew her short sword, and she hastened ahead keeping an eye on the water but also the path before her. It was a narrow trail, with water on one side and thick growth on the other. Tree roots bulged out, creeping over the wet dirt like crawling fingers trying to trip those who dared to walk the path. Snakes were common in places such as this, some deadly, and oftentimes they lay on the bare earth to bake in the sun.

There were none today though, and she quickened her pace even more. The sky was bright above, and sweat began to slick her face. This drew the flies more, and she tossed her hair angrily but they settled down around her patiently again.

Soon, she reached the end of this section of the path and the lake to her left receded and was replaced by bogland. The band of trees to her right thickened, and it was into them that the path turned.

It grew dark quickly, yet the shade was no cooler. If anything, it felt hotter here because the air was moist and unmoving. The ground was firm though, and few things dangerous dwelled in the woods of the fen. The mosquitoes were as bad as ever, but the flies did not like the dark.

She went forward, angling her way toward where her companions would be. It was a relief to get closer to them, and she would feel better once the burden of her news had been delivered. If something happened to her before she reached them, her people would know nothing of the threat that faced them.

It was easy enough to traverse the wood. The ground was firm, and there was little undergrowth to hinder her. Yet this was one of the few places where the land rose into a kind of hill, and that slowed her progress.

The wood was silent around her, and then she realized it was *too* silent. Nothing stirred. No bird in the tops of the trees, nor any smaller beast that skittered among the leaf mold betrayed its presence. The silence was heavy, and her heart began to thud in her chest.

She was being watched, and she knew it. How she was sure of that, she did not know. But her instincts rarely let her down. Life in the fen had trained her well, and her role among the leng-fah had sharpened that training to a razor's edge. She knew, and she did not like it.

It might be one of her own people, but no signal had been given. Perhaps it was some scout of the Soaring

Eagle band, but she doubted that. They would have followed her rather than be ahead of her somewhere.

No, this was someone else. But who?

Again, she drew her short sword and crept forward, her every sense alive to the woods around her. She dared not delay bringing her news to her leader, but she dared not go forward any faster. Whoever it was that hid from her was greatly skilled, otherwise she would have detected where they were already, and that meant they were dangerous.

3. The Mark of Death

The air was still. The wood was silent. Nothing seemed to stir in all the world, but Shar felt her heart race.

If she were being watched, and she knew that she was, then drawing her sword had signaled she was aware of it. Her enemy, for no friend would remain hidden, would thus know that she was on the alert and be even more cautious.

Shar stood still, her gaze seeking out every possible hiding spot in the vicinity. There were many, and she noted them all. Nor did she fail to tilt her head upward and study the twisted branches of the trees above. Yet she saw nothing.

It could not go on. She had someplace else to be, yet nor could she run the gauntlet here and risk her life to a thrusted blade in the back as she ventured forward.

"I know you're there," she said, and she made her voice firm. "Come out and show yourself. I'll not go forward, but if I must I'll call my friends here. They are within earshot."

In truth, she was not sure they were. She still had some distance to go, and this thick wood would stifle any call she made.

The hush grew deeper, and more menacing. There was no answer save for the silence itself, loud enough it seemed to burst her eardrums. Yet her words, though they had failed to bring the enemy out, were also a subterfuge to cover her next move.

She had said she would not go forward, but that was a lie to deceive her opponent. With a sudden spring she raced ahead, leaped an old decaying tree trunk that had fallen over the path, and then swerved to the side, rolled and came up to her feet again with her back to a tree and her sword before her.

Her opponent had not expected that, and was revealed. A hooded man leaped at her from where he had been hidden behind a tree trunk, and a sword was in one hand and a knife in the other. It was not a combination of weapons that Shar had seen before, and that was strange.

The man came at her, swift as any attack she had ever seen. Her sword flashed out, deflecting his main strike, but his knife nearly disemboweled her.

All around them the wood was no longer silent. Now it erupted in the clash of steel against steel and the heavy breaths of hard exertion. The soft earth was churned, and half-decayed branches and twigs snapped underfoot.

Shar felt a surge of fear. This man fought like none she had seen before, and he was both swift and strong. She gave way, albeit slowly, tempting him into an overconfident stroke, but he would have none of it. Every trap she set for him, he saw and avoided.

Yet as the moments passed her fear subsided. This man was good. He was the best she had ever seen, and yet, even so, and despite all his attempts, he had not been able to kill her.

He was wary now, and though she could see little of his face beneath the hood she saw his jaw clenched in determination and from time to time an intense look on his dark eyes when they were suddenly revealed in a patch of broken light. He was giving this his all, and yet still he could not kill her.

That gave her confidence. The fight had moved farther into the trees now, but there was a patch of clear ground to the side. She edged toward this, for it was lighter here and she sensed that her opponent preferred the dark. He had hidden in it, and it helped hide the flashing of his knife which she now knew was a greater threat to her than his sword.

The battle went on, and it was one such as Shar had never fought before. It was to the death. She knew this in her heart, though no word had been spoken. Her opponent was unrelenting, and so must she also be if she were to survive.

She saw him better now, and all the more so after his hood fell back when he leaped sideways to avoid a stroke she delivered. His hair was short, and his cheekbones high below a cruel gaze. It was not just cruel though. It was the hard gaze of one who had seen much and lived through it. It was the gaze of a man who had seen others die, and who likely had been the cause.

He was older too, yet no less supple for it. His skill was the best she had ever seen, and his tactics slightly different as well. Strangest of all though, not only was he not of the Fen Wolves, he was not of the Soaring Eagle Clan either. He wore no eagle feather in either a cap, nor through a headband as they sometimes did. He was a stranger, from a strange tribe, and that unnerved her. What was he doing here? And why attack her?

Her arm was weary now, and her shoulder burned. She showed none of that. To display weakness was to give the enemy hope, which in turn would stoke his own reserves of strength. Yet she detected tiredness in him also. Unless that was a trap intended to fool her into attacking without enough caution.

Their blades rang in the silence of the woods. Their footfalls were soft in the glade where one or the other of them would spill their blood, and life, into the soil. Yet neither, for all their effort, could obtain an advantage over the other.

But no battle could continue for long without a victor. One mistake was all it took to fall, and sooner or later one of them must make that error.

Shar felt no fear now. What would be would be, and if it were her destiny to die this day, so be it. Yet she believed that her fate would be different, and that she had more, so much more, to offer her people than she had yet given.

The warrior before her swayed to the side, and his sword arced up as if to strike. But it was with his knife that he struck instead, using his sword more as a shield to protect his head. Shar had never seen the maneuver before, but she had quickly come to know this man and his methods, and to understand the way he used his sword to draw attention while the knife stealthily probed for her life.

She did not back away. Rather, she stepped to the side and kicked out with her foot at his knee. Two could play this game of surprises. The blow struck hard, but she had not quite got the angle right to damage and collapse the joint as she intended. So it was that her enemy managed to retreat and avoid the follow-up sword strike that would have killed him.

They studied each other for a moment in silence, and for the first time since the fight had begun the ring of blade against blade ceased. Slowly the man raised his arms, holding both sword and knife high. The sleeves of his tunic fell down his arms, exposing the skin. What Shar saw there sent a chill through her blood.

A snake was tattooed in black ink winding down each forearm, and it spat crimson venom toward the man's wrist. Shar knew who this man was now, and from what tribe he hailed. He was an Ahat, an assassin, as all members of that tribe spent their entire lives training to be, men, women and children all. None knew where their homeland was, but their presence always meant death for

29

their intended victim. The snake sign was their totem, and it was the mark of death.

He leaped at her again, his sword flashing with blinding speed. She reeled back, stunned by the revelation of who he was and the ferociousness of his attack.

Twice she stumbled, and twice she came near to death, but her skill did not desert her, and she fended off his blows, again and again, until at last the ferocity left them and he resumed the more normal strategy of probing here and there for a weakness, like water trying to slowly seep through a crack rather than a flood taking all before it and spending itself quickly.

She moved to the side where there was a slight slope, and she took the uphill part of it. She tried to think only of the fight, but her mind raced over other thoughts. What was he doing here? Had he intended to kill her? Or had she merely forced him into action when he was only trying to remain hidden? Most of all, she wondered if he was in any way connected to the raid of the Soaring Eagles. He was not with them, and yet his and their presence at the same time must otherwise be a great coincidence.

He must be here to kill *someone*, and she could think of only two possibilities for that. Neither would she allow while she had breath left in her body, yet the awe in which the Ahat were held by all the Cheng peoples quickened doubt within her. How could she defeat one such as him?

With a deft movement she deflected a blow and sent a riposte slashing back toward his neck. He jumped back with a curse, and his dark eyes fixed on her with hatred. It was the first sound he had uttered, and it suddenly made him seem less legend and more human.

Shar stalked toward him, her sword held loosely in her hand and her body relaxing into the fight. In the momentary pause of blows she realized something. The man had deliberately shown the snake tattoos to her. It had been no accident, and now she understood why he had done so. It was an attempt to intimidate her.

Her blood boiled at that, for she would be intimidated by no one. Yet she held herself in check. Should she allow emotion to control her now she might die because of some rash stroke.

She was glad of her control, for like a shadow to the first thought came another. Why had he tried to intimidate her with fear? There was only one reason. He felt fear himself, and his skills had failed him. He had tried to kill her and could not. Now, he resorted to trickery.

Shar grinned at him. If he wanted to play with her mind, then she would return the favor.

"Death is upon you, assassin, and my sword will deliver justice for your crimes."

She saw his eyes widen at that, and she knew her words had struck home as surely as any blade. With a cry he leaped at her, but she was calm and ready. His blade hissed through the air, and she stepped forward to meet it, nimbly turning the strike away from her with a deflection and then stepping in again.

But it was the pommel of her sword that she struck him with rather than the blade. He was caught by surprise, and the force of her blow was great for she drove all her bodyweight into it.

The assassin staggered back, and he did not even see the next strike. Her blade whipped around, and she arced it at his neck. It passed through, and a thin red line appeared against his skin. He made to scream, but no sound came, and then blood gushed out of his throat. He fell to his knees, and Shar stepped back. A dying warrior could be more dangerous than one who thought he might yet live.

A moment he remained where he was, one hand pressed hard against his throat, but then he dropped the

31

sword and pressed the other there also. Yet even as he did so his eyes changed, and he toppled slowly forward and lay still.

He was dead, and Shar was alive. It was her first kill, and she did not like it even if it had been forced upon her. Pity welled up within her, but at the same time came a rush of relief. She was *alive*, and her future and all that she might yet be stretched out before her like an untraveled road that beckoned.

She took a few moments to calm herself and regain her breath. Too much had happened here, and she understood little of it, still less how she felt about it. But that must wait for consideration at another time. For the moment, duty called and she had other tasks.

First was to search the corpse that lay before her. She did so, looking at the serpent tattoos initially to confirm she had not imagined them. But they were there, and they still sent a shiver down her spine. She pulled the dead man's sleaves down quickly.

On his body she found several things of interest. First was a leather pouch. She carefully opened this, and found it contained several smaller pouches. She opened the strings of each, then drew them tight again quickly. Each contained dried herbs that smelled strange. She was not sure what they were, but she suspected they were various poisons. The deadly arts of the assassins were wider than mere swords and knives.

Next she found a length of string, but realized it was actually a metal wire. Of such devices she had heard, and knew it for a means of garroting people. She looked down on the body, and felt less guilt at her part in his death. This was a device that killed from behind, hidden and unexpected in the dark. It was not a warrior's way of fighting.

There was another pouch with five gold coins. It was more gold than Shar had ever seen at once, possibly more gold than even the clan chief himself possessed. On this she thought hard. It could help her, and it could benefit her village. But at length she put the coins back in their purse. She had no wish to profit from the slaying of this man.

There was another device hidden inside his tunic. It was a length of woody plant material. She thought it was some kind of rush, but it was larger than the ones she was used to. It was neatly cut on both ends and over a foot in length. It was hollow, but she could not decide what use it was put to. Then it occurred to her that it would enable an assassin to hide in a body of water and yet breathe. A strange thing, yet perhaps one that might come in handy. This she kept.

Last of all she found a slip of parchment. It was creased and worn, barely larger than one of her fingers. Yet it had writing on it in an angled script. She was one of the few in the fens who could read, thanks to her grandmother's teaching, yet this was a script she had never seen before, and it puzzled her. But there was a seal at the end of the writing, and it was a single serpent, jaws wide and without venom as on the man's arm. She did not know what it signified, but it might be important, so she folded it and placed it in one of her pockets.

There was only one more thing to do. The body must be hidden, for where there was one assassin there might be another. It was best they did not know their comrade was dead, for that would raise questions. Who in a poor clan like this had the skill to defeat an Ahat? It was a question that was better to never be asked. And any villager who stumbled over the body might ask the same question.

Shar was not ready to answer such questions yet, so she picked up the body and began to look for a lower patch of ground where mud would hide it. And her secrets.

4. The Leng-fah

Even on the higher ground on which the wood grew, it did not take Shar long to find a boggy area. Having done so, she cast the body into it.

A moment she paused, while it slowly sank in the mud, and she thought of death and that one day it would come to her. She spoke no words, but remained silent a moment, head bowed, in respect of the passing of a life. It did not matter what she thought of the man. The death of a person deserved that much. At least to her mind, though she knew that some rejoiced in the downfall of an enemy.

When this was done, she swiftly carried on, and she found a way through the wood and to lower land again where there were less trees. The sun was hot on the back of her neck when she passed into open patches, but going farther down a slope the trees closed in again and the ground grew wet and hard to tread without the risk of becoming trapped.

Yet she knew her way here, and soon found what she sought. A path had been made, and it was concealed so that few might find it unless they knew the signs that marked its presence or had come this way before. It was of felled logs, short and laid horizontally over the mud.

She eyed the path warily, but then moved onto the logs at a slowed her pace. They were slippery, and they covered dangerous ground. To fall might be to sink into the earth and never be able to find footing to push herself back up on the track.

The trail did not last long. It was just enough to get a traveler over the worst patch, and nothing more. Yet it saved a long walk around. There were many such laid paths in the fens, and they were useful but dangerous. They were not always in good repair and there were stories of those who trusted them only to find that the logs sank under their weight and they could go neither forward nor back, but only down.

She came to the other side and raced on. She did not fear another assassin or any other enemy. No one could predict the route she traveled, but at times she came to a sudden stop and listed for any sign of pursuit. There was none.

From somewhere ahead came the sharp cry of a moorhen, eerie and strange as it always was. Yet to Shar, it was stranger than it seemed for it was no bird at all that made the nose. It was one of her own people, and it was a question. *We are here. Where are you?*

It meant they were worried about her, for they had expected her sooner than this. Almost she gave a reply, but she chose not to. The less this means of communication was used the better. That reduced the chances anyone could discern what it was.

But she was close, too. That call had been loud, and it would not be long at all before she reached her companions.

Speeding ahead, she noticed that the forest began to thin and turn into wetlands meshed with patches of grassland. Still, there were quite a few trees, and she kept to these and the cover they offered.

She slowed, for she had come to the place where she expected her friends to be. There was no sign of them, but that did not mean they were not there. Walking slowly now, she studied the landscape carefully.

It was not long before she spotted someone hidden in the canopy of a tree. A little to the left and behind a stand of ferns she also saw a slight movement. There would be other lookouts, but she failed to spot them.

Yet evidently the person in the tree had spotted her and passed on a signal, for she saw Argash, the leader of her patrol, emerge from behind a bush and beckon her forward.

Shar entered a small clearing, surrounded by bushes. The grass was green here, and cropped low by the swamp deer that loved places such as these.

There were no deer here now though, only her people, and they had worried expressions. They had read much into her warning, and they had been right to do so.

"What did you discover?" Argash asked.

With speed and efficiency, Shar related to him all that she had learned while the others listened, their expressions stony, but their eyes revealing a hint of the emotions beneath.

She left out no important detail, but time was slipping by and she recounted events with a minimum of words. At least, those events that concerned the Soaring Eagles. Of the Ahat, she said nothing at all. Nor the unreadable writing on the parchment. There were some things that she kept hidden even from those she trusted with her life, and there were few indeed of those. Of those present, Argash was the only one.

When she was done, Argash gave her a searching look. He could not know that she had not told him all, for she had no wounds that spoke of her being in a fight. Yet she had taken longer to reach them than she should have, and that would not have escaped his attention. Yet he asked nothing more.

"You did well," he said.

He turned and beckoned over two other warriors. These were his friends, or at least those whose advice he most often listened to. But he did not dismiss Shar, and she stood with them.

"What do you suggest?" he asked them.

"We must return to the chief as quickly as possible," the first man answered quickly and with confidence in his opinion. "He'll gather many warriors and then we'll return and teach these Soaring Eagles a lesson they'll not forget."

Argash looked thoughtful and turned to the second man. "Your counsel?"

This man was somewhat older, and he took his time to answer. "Each choice is dangerous. But we do have options. We can confront these intruders and try to stymie their plans. If we don't, there are many small villages that will pay a price in blood. Yet it seems they are double our strength. Prudence dictates we can do nothing save alert the chief and await reinforcements."

Argash did not look happy, and Shar did not blame him. It was a hard choice, and she did not envy him having to make it. Yet she had her own ideas, but bided her time to speak them.

In the glade the flies buzzed and from afar came the sounds of the swamp. Argash creased his brow in thought, but at length turned to Shar.

"You've seen the enemy firsthand. What do you advise?"

It was not the first time he had asked for her counsel. She was younger than most here, and female, which not many of the leng-fah were. But Argash had disregarded that. He was one who rewarded intelligence wherever he found it, and played no favorites. Shar wished there were more like him.

She drew herself up, but spoke without passion. This was a time for reason and not emotion. Lives depended on what she said.

5. Ambush

Shar answered quickly. "This is my advice," she said, holding the gaze of Argash. "The enemy outnumber us, and can cause great harm to our people. Yet they don't outnumber us _yet_. If we move swiftly, we can catch up to that first column before they meet the second. Then the fight will be even in terms of numbers, but the terrain, being in the fen, will be to our advantage."

Argash raised an eyebrow at that, but gave no reply.

"What then of the chief?" the younger of the others interrupted. "If we are killed, then who will send him word?"

Shar had thought of that. "We can spare one runner to return to him and give him all this news. That will not weaken our force too much, and that way we lose nothing, but, perhaps, gain much."

Still, Argash answered nothing, but the older man spoke.

"What you say may be true, but what if we don't reach the first force before it joins to the second? And even if we do, that still leaves the second force free to work evil. We cannot fight it after tackling the first. We will have lost men and be tired."

The fen was still once more, or maybe Shar had ceased to listen to it. All that mattered for the moment was this debate.

"We either reach the first column in time, or we don't," she replied. "If we don't, we can choose not to attack and we lose nothing. But I think we can reach them. In the fens we travel twice as quick as they do. As for the second group … I have a plan for them too. But first things first. Time is running out on us, and every moment we delay makes our task harder."

Argash scratched his chin. "A bold plan, Shar."

She knew it was. She also knew it was the right one, and that it had the best chance of protecting the small villages and communities that would otherwise be massacred. But that did not mean it would be followed.

There was silence now while Argash considered the options he had been given, and no doubt considered how the chief and the Fen Wolf shaman would react. They had adopted a policy of reducing tension with their aggressive neighbors, and retaliating to crimes with the minimal force necessary. That was a mistake, and it only encouraged further aggression. But Argash might face consequences if he went against that policy now, no matter how brazen this attack from their enemy was.

The silence in the clearing was profound, and all the eyes of the leng-fah were on their leader. But his decision being made, he broke into rapid action.

"You," he said, pointing to the newest recruit to the band, "hasten to the chief and tell him all that has transpired. Tell him we go to attack this warband that has entered our territory. Run!"

The man leaped up and ran away without a word, but Argash was already giving more commands. "You," he said, picking two members of the patrol. "Scout a little ahead of us with Shar and lead us to this first column." He indicated Shar to go with them, and he spoke to the rest of the band. "Follow their lead. We march to battle! Have courage, and remember these fens our ours. We know them better than the enemy, and their every danger is a friend to us and a trap to them. Remember, and be brave!"

The patrol surged to their feet and Shar was already hastening ahead with the two other scouts. They fanned

41

out as they went, and Shar took the point position in the center. She would lead them for she knew best where the enemy would be.

Time had passed them by, and perhaps too much of it. Shar sought to make that up, and she scouted ahead at a rapid pace. Her two companions kept in hearing range, and they communicated now and then by various calls of the wildlife of the fen. So too they communicated to those who followed a little way back. This kept them all together and in the proper formation just like a hunting pack of fen wolves, from whom the leng-fah had learned the trick.

The day was wearing on. The noontime sun was rising, and the fen was approaching its hottest and most unpleasant period. The mosquitoes were lessened, but the flies were at their worst. Sweat trickled down Shar's back, and her palms were wet with moisture. She preferred the dusk to the middle of the day, but by dusk this day she may be dead, and those with her, if her advice turned out to be bad.

But it was not. She knew that in her heart. Their job was to protect the villages of the fen, and this was the way to best do it.

They came to higher ground again, and there was a welcome breeze on her face. Yet they must by now be getting close to the enemy column, and she was careful to find a way forward where no one who followed would be exposed to view.

The height did not last long, and soon they plunged down an embankment into lower and boggier ground. Shar could not see it, but there was a village a mile or so to the west. No sound came from that direction, nor any sign of smoke. She believed all was well there, and she veered a little to the east hoping to cross the trail of those she hunted.

She found it sooner than she expected. It was plain to see, and it was fresh. They had gained ground on the enemy quicker than expected. Most likely the Soaring Eagles had slowed down. By now they must have noticed the loss of their rear scout, and that would have worried them, all the more so for not knowing if he had come to harm by some accident or had been killed by an elusive enemy who followed them.

The tracks of the enemy swerved around the low-lying ground, and Shar fell back to speak with Argash.

"The Soaring Eagles don't know what we do," she advised him. "They circle this area, but we can cut straight through, instead of following, and get to the other side ahead of them. There we can rest briefly, and wait in ambush."

Argash made his decision quickly. "Let it be so," he agreed.

Shar went to the fore again, and led the leng-fah onward. They were bunched up closer now, for this was dangerous territory and there was no chance of the enemy waylaying them.

She picked the way forward carefully. Wet, boggy and dangerous as this area looked, there was still a firm path across it. This was signaled by marks that none could read save leng-fah. Where there were trees, branches had been lopped on one side and not the other to give direction. Rocks lay on the ground, and they gave a message too. Reeds were bent over, and even in places certain herbage had been cultivated so that any time of year, either by foliage or their flowers, a message was given for those with the skill to read it.

Shar missed none of them, and she used also her experience as a denizen of Tsarin Fen that only a native dweller could possess. Since she could walk, she had navigated the perils of the wetlands, and that was something no outsider could ever match. So it was that she led them all to the drier ground on the other side as the noonday sun began to lower in the sky.

With care, she and the other two scouts sought sign of the enemy. There was none. No tracks could they find, nor even hear them approach. All was well, unless they had altered the course she thought they intended to take.

The main body of the leng-fah were called through. Argash positioned them well, for half of them took the well-covered ground on the edge of the wetlands that was grown thick with rushes as a hiding place, and the other half found concealment opposite in a stand of hoary oaks, half rotting and leaning over. Between lay the path the enemy would traverse, if indeed they came this way.

Yet of the Soaring Eagles there was no sign. Shar began to worry, for if she had been mistaken about where the enemy must come then it would require trying to find their trail again and then following. The day would be spent before they could hope to catch up with them, and all the while the chances grew that the enemy would meet their second force and grow too strong to engage.

The long minutes passed by, and Shar felt the weight of them as an eternity. Yet at least the leng-fah were resting, and that was a good thing. They had traveled hard and far, and a respite would see them fight better when that time came, if it did.

Shar looked up from where she was positioned in the rushes near Argash. A kestrel hovered there, then veered away to another spot to hover again. It sought prey on the ground below, but it was not the only hunter in this part of the fens. Suddenly, it dropped down and disappeared from sight.

Even as the kestrel was lost from view, three ducks burst from the trees hundreds of feet away in the direction

44

the path they surrounded came from. But nothing else was seen or heard.

Yet at length a lone man came into view, walking carefully and studying the landscape with suspicion. At last the enemy had come, for even from here Shar could see the eagle feather sticking up from his headband.

The leng-fah were silent, for they were skilled at their profession. Not a reed moved, nor any indication of their presence was revealed. Shar was proud of them. They faced mortal danger now, but their training came to the fore despite the threat of impending battle.

Soon, the enemy scout approached. Behind him followed the rest of the Soaring Eagles. Shar was surprised at how small the gap was between them, but she guessed the disappearance of the earlier scout was responsible for this.

The scout was close enough now that she could see his face, and he walked down the path with a frown and his hand close to his sword hilt. His eyes darted nervously two and fro, and he seemed to have to force himself to take each step.

For a little while Shar worried there were other scouts they had not seen, but there was no sign of this. The enemy came on, worried but unwitting of the trap set to close about them.

It was a tense moment, but the scout went past the ambush and did not detect it. He disappeared behind some trees, but he was marked for death. The leng-fah farthest down that side would see to him when the ambush was sprung. That way he could not return to help his comrades, or worse, go on to warn the second column of Soaring Eagles.

The main body of the enemy came down the path now, and they were between the two sides of the ambush. With a sudden war cry, Argash leaped up from his hiding place and flung a knife that took a man in the neck. This was the signal for the leng-fah to act, and like a storm that burst from a cloudless sky they unleashed unexpected chaos.

The little path in the fens became a trail of blood and horror as though Death itself, terrible and unexpected, trod it implacably.

Shar saw other knives fly, and then she was up and running, her short sword in hand. To her right, Argash engaged an enemy warrior, but there was little battle there. Argash was a good swordsman, and the other unprepared. In a moment the Soaring Eagle warrior was falling to the ground and blood pulsing from an arterial wound in his thigh.

The crash of steel and the cries of enemy dismay rang out, and Shar engaged her own warrior. He was an older man, approaching middle age. Scars ran down his face, and he wore two eagle feathers through his tight leather cap. He was no doubt a veteran of many battles, and unlike many of his companions he made no sound as they squared off.

With a powerful thrust the old man tried to disembowel her. Shar answered that with a deflection, for her slighter build meant that invariably she sought to redirect the strength of her opponents than to resist them with force. And having done so, her blade whipped back and tore out his throat. He toppled back; surprise etched on his face.

Shar surged forward seeking another enemy. But they were all engaged or dying. The ambush had been launched so swiftly and at such close range that the Soaring Eagles never had much chance. In moments they were all dead, and silence descended once more over the fens.

Argash looked around at his patrol. "Anyone wounded?" he asked.

Few were, and those were only slight injuries. But one of their own lay dead, an enemy sword still protruding from his chest. Argash cursed quietly, withdrew the sword and closed the man's staring eyes.

One of the patrol came trotting down the path and Argash called out to him. "Their scout?"

"Dead," came the reply.

That was a relief to Shar. She had a plan for what must come next, but it would fail had the scout escaped to give warning to the other Soaring Eagles.

They moved a little farther down the track so as not to be next to the slain. There they bandaged wounds and Argash took a full account of the injuries and began to assess what to do next.

Shar stitched a cut a man had received to his arm. It was deep, and it required many loops of her thread, but the wound seemed clean and she used some herbs on it that all the leng-far carried for such purposes. They were supposed to help fight infection, but she was not convinced of their efficacy. She had also used dar shun, deftly finding pressure points and triggering them to help dull the pain, without the man noticing what she did.

As she worked, her mind raced over other matters. Things had gone well so far, and her plan had succeeded with as little loss as could possibly be expected. Had she not suggested it, she did not think Argash would have enacted anything like it. He was a good man, but his leadership was never bold. Yet he had, despite advice to the contrary, followed her strategy. He had faith in her, and they had a good relationship. Nor was he a supporter of the shamans. There were others in the group who were though, and she did not doubt that had the plan failed both she and Argash would have suffered consequences.

Even as she thought of such things, Argash came over to her after he finished bandaging a bloody wound to a man's calf muscle.

"What next?" he asked. "You said you had an idea once we were done here, and I'm ready to hear it."

Shar took a deep breath. Argash was certainly not bold, but this next step she would advise would be even bolder than her original idea.

6. It Will Go Badly

The rest of the leng-fah slowly gathered around, and Shar spoke.

"We have removed one threat to the fens, but not the other. The second column of the Soaring Eagles still remains to be dealt with."

The younger man whom Argash sometimes received advice from spoke up. He was related to the chief, but Shar had never known that to bestow him with any great intelligence.

"You wish us to take them on? It's impossible! We've already fought a battle and our number is reduced by two."

Shar shrugged. "If you say so, then no doubt you believe it. But difficult is not the same as impossible. The first is overcome with courage or endurance. The second can never be overcome if it is created by a lack of will to try."

The younger man reddened, and would have replied, but Argash raised his hand. "We have no time for this. Speak plainly, Shar."

Shar gestured back toward where the dead Soaring Eagles lay.

"Those we have already beaten offer us a means of defeating their comrades also. Do not each of them have an eagle feather? Can we not take those, and wear them ourselves? And if we do, we might get close to the enemy before they realize they have been deceived and attack them with the advantage of surprise. That will compensate for our lowered numbers and tiredness."

There was silence then, for it truly was a bold plan, yet one that had the seeds of success in it. But any mischance could still see them fight a larger force that was fresh, without an advantage.

Argash bowed his head in thought. Shar did not push him with her plan. She knew the seriousness of what she proposed. Without doubt, more of the Fen Wolves would die and responsibility for that would rest on him.

They could not hope to find an opportunity to set an ambush as had been done here. They had known where the enemy was and the terrain had favored them. Tackling the second column was different because they would not be coming at it from behind but head on, and they might meet suddenly and unexpectedly.

Argash, she knew, despite being a cautious man, felt as she did. If they did not act, then innocent villagers would die. No doubt some already had, for the second column had likely attacked an outlying settlement just like the first. The responsibility for any further deaths would be on him, and he knew it. Nevertheless, he arrived at his decision quickly.

"You and you," he said, signaling to two warriors, "retrieve the eagle feathers and headbands we'll need."

They moved off quickly, but there was doubt on their faces.

Argash looked subdued. "This really is a bold plan, Shar."

"I know it," she answered. "But would you leave villages unprotected until the chief gets here with more men."

"No, I would not."

Looking around, it was clear to Shar though that not everyone shared this view. Some of the leng-fah muttered to each other. She could not hear, but she knew they were unhappy. In truth, she could not blame them. They were going into great danger now, and without doubt some of them would die. It was on Argash's head because he was leader, but it was on her head also. But it was their job to protect the fens, and she was at as much risk as they were. And the guilt of any who died because they did not take action would weigh on her more strongly than the risk of death. That was her though, but she knew that some others did not have that same sense of responsibility.

The sun was beginning to drop in the sky, and the shadows lengthened. Yet they soon wore an eagle feather, most through headbands but some sticking up from tight leather caps. They sprang forward, Shar leading the way as she had previously with the two other scouts.

She did not know exactly where to go. The enemy scout she had interrogated claimed not to know the meeting place for the two columns, and he was likely telling the truth. Yet the first column had been consistent in the direction they took, and had only veered from that when the terrain interfered. Then, as soon as possible, they headed back to that same course.

Her every sense alert, she continued on. But she thought as she walked, and she tried to put herself in the mind of the enemy. It was a basic skill of scouting, and it was useful. The better she could think like them, the more chance of predicting their actions.

What place would they choose to meet? It could be anywhere, and for a Fen Wolf one place would be as good as another. Yet for a stranger in this land, would they not seek an obvious place? Would they not head for a landmark of some sort that could be easily found?

Straightaway she paused and looked up. On the path that they were headed on there was one such place, and one that they could reach by nightfall. Certainty gripped her as she saw it: a hill, if such it could be called in these lowlands. It was covered by trees and offered good concealment. It was defendable. It was easily located, and most of all it was the kind of place that could be found by two separate groups that were unfamiliar with the territory, yet might have heard accounts of the Tsarin Fen from those who had traveled it.

It also occurred to her that the leng-fah would be at a disadvantage. The enemy would likely reach the crest of the hill before them, and they would hold the high ground when it came to a battle. Also, from that height, they would see them coming, even if they thought them the friends they expected.

The sun fell in the sky, and the shadows lengthened. The feel of the fen changed, for it was always very different at night from what it was at day, and dawn and dusk were different again. Some called the fen the fourfold land because it changed greatly all the time, yet others maintained that reference was to solid land and water as well as light and dark of being within the trees or without. As far as Shar was concerned, they were all right.

She led them as best she could, seeking a way to offer concealment from any who looked down from the hill. She doubted they could remain hidden, but still the attempt must be made.

Soon they climbed the hill itself, and she made the call of a swamp cat. It was a warning that she expected danger ahead, and to be ready.

Of the enemy, there was no sign. Yet she did smell smoke in the air. Perhaps it was a hidden campfire of the Soaring Eagles. Or it might be from a village, for there were several close enough. But she thought it was neither. The smoke smelled old to her, and she thought it might be from a raid last night or this morning. She hoped she was wrong.

Toward the crest she slowed down and allowed the rest of the leng-fah to catch up. They were within sight of her now, only a few dozen paces back, yet still there was no sign of anyone else on the hill with them.

That changed swiftly. She heard a noise and drew her sword. In a moment, several Soaring Eagle tribesmen came out from behind the trees and challenged her. They made a sign with their hands, and she knew it was some kind of password but she did not know what response to give.

There was only one thing to do. She staggered, and held a hand to her body as though wounded. All the while she kept going forward, and the leng-fah came up quickly behind.

The Soaring Eagles seemed in doubt. More of them came out from behind the trees, some with their blades drawn and others not bothering, evidently seeing no further than the eagle feathers on the newcomers' heads as confirmation that friends were at hand.

"Give the signal!" one of the men shouted, and he raised his sword in a fighting position.

Shar gave no answer. Instead she staggered again, but this time she fell. Yet even as she hit the ground she rolled forward and then leaped up to attack, and the war cry of the leng-fah came like a wave from behind her.

For a moment she fought by herself. To the sides her two fellow scouts also rushed forward to attack. She faced three men, swinging wildly at her, and then the leng-fah rolled forward and crashed into the enemy.

A battle broke out. This was no ambush as the previous fight had been, but the advantage was with Shar and her tribe. Yet more and more of the Soaring Eagles poured out from where they must have been resting beyond the trees. It was a bigger column than the first had been, and the leng-fah were outnumbered.

Shar killed one man, and the rush of her comrades temporarily blocked her from the enemy. Then a Fen

Wolf fell near her, his head hacked away by a giant of a man with a heavy broadsword. This warrior screamed in triumph, and then swung at Shar.

He was too strong for her. But all her life she had fought stronger men. She weaved to the side and her own blade flashed out to take him in the groin. He saw the attack though, and for all his size he could move quickly. He leaned back, deflecting her blow with a backhanded strike of his heavier blade.

She felt the force of that parry even if it was only a deflection, and the thrum of it ran up her arm. In turn, she skipped back a pace as the warrior circled his blade into an overhead strike. Had she been quick enough she could have killed him then while his body was unguarded. Perhaps she *was* quick enough, yet even if the man were dead the weight of that blow would still topple down upon her.

She raised her own blade lengthwise, but at an angle, and leaned to the opposite side. The warrior's sword struck with tremendous force, yet even as rain ran from a pitched roof so too his blade skidded to the side.

Shar darted in. This time she lunged at the man's belly. The tip of her blade pierced the flesh there, but only just. He nimbly jumped back, and she followed him, turning her lunge into a skip and an upward strike intended to take him under the chin.

The warrior dropped his shoulder and deflected her blade with it. It was a desperate tactic, yet it worked and it left her vulnerable. Again the mighty sword crashed down, and this time she was out of position and unable to raise her weapon in time to redirect the blow. Nor did she have time to jump back to safety.

Death was as close to Shar now as it had been facing the assassin earlier in the day. And she was tired while this man was fresh. Yet she was skilled, and confident in her ability. Had she not been trained in secret by her grandmother, who had taught her dar shun that no one else in the fens knew? Was she not trained to face the greatest warriors in the land?

With a scream that might have been of fear, or of the wild joy of battle, she attempted neither of the defenses that would come to the mind of others and see her dead for lack of time. Instead, she dropped low and propelled herself forward against the man's legs.

Even as a mountain must fall should the earth heave, so tumbled the warrior, and he toppled over her in a ruin of tangled limbs, his sword strike being forgotten as he sought to break his fall. But Shar was already moving, and she scrambled around and thrust with the tip of her blade into the man's neck from behind. She pinned him there as he convulsed, his legs kicking out and striking her, but she thought he was already dead.

Weary as she had seldom been, and sick at heart from inflicting death, Shar rose up, her sword dripping blood, and looked around for another enemy. There was none.

The last of the fighting was ending some thirty paces away to her left. All around her were the dead warriors of the Soaring Eagle Clan, yet many Fen Wolves lay there also. These were men who had died because of her plan. She mourned them. She knew she might easily have been one of them. Even so, what else could have been done that would have cost less lives?

One half of the Fen Wolves were dead. Only a handful remained, yet Argash was one of them, and she took heart in that. He was a good man, and of them all the closest to a friend. He came over to her, his face white and his hand clasped to a wound on his leg.

"It is done," he said. "And we have won. If at a high cost."

Shar drew out some cloth that she carried that would serve as a bandage for him.

"We both knew it would be a hard fight, and that some of us would fall."

"Aye. I knew. Yet still, it seems so needless to me. So many lives lost, and for what? We could have done nothing else though. But why did the Soaring Eagles have to come at all?"

It was a good question, and she had no answer to that. It was the way of the land, and all over the single empire that once had been, many, many clans fought with each other and died. All for nothing. All over petty squabbles. All at the behest of the shamans who could stop it if they chose. Yet a divided empire was easier to rule from the cover of shadows.

There was a commotion to the side. One of the enemy warriors had been found alive. He may have been rendered unconscious by a blow to the head, or he may have feigned death to try to escape it. Yet he had been found out, and now he tried to scramble away from the ring of Fen Wolves closing on him, swords raised.

"Wait!" cried Shar, and she strode over. Then she hesitated and looked at Argash. "May I speak?"

"Speak," he commanded.

She turned to the enemy warrior. "I don't know why the Soaring Eagles came to the fen. I don't know what reasons were given. But tell me if I'm wrong in this. It was at the behest of your shaman, was it not?"

The man nodded. "It was," he answered.

"The shamans breed violence between the clans," she replied. "Always they have, and always they will. Yet that cycle can end. We can make a start now." She turned to Argash. "Let this man return to his homeland. Let him tell his people that we are not the enemy, but we will defend what is ours. Let him go, or do we now execute prisoners?"

Argash remained silent while he thought. "Go!" he said at length to the man. "We do not murder here, in the fens. Go, but never come back with a sword in your hand, for death will surely find you then."

The man ran off, but some of the Fen Wolves seemed angry. Argash silenced them with a look, but then took Shar aside to speak in private.

"No true warrior of the Fen Wolves commits murder," he said, "so my decision cannot be questioned. Yet you spoke rashly. You must know that your words will be reported back to the shaman, and I fear things will go badly for you when we return."

7. The Blood of Your Ancestor

Shar walked along the main path of her village, the largest of the many villages in Tsarin Fen. Yet there were still only a hundred or so huts here, and poverty was everywhere.

It had been a bleak journey back. The remaining members of the leng-fah were grim. They had all lost friends. A few of them blamed her for it, and they were sullen. Along the way they had been found by scouts of the chief. These had not stayed with them though, but being fresh hastened back with news of what had happened.

The chief had mobilized his warriors. It could not be called an army, yet it was some hundred men. It was a tenth of the full strength of the Fen Wolves though, and it was a force to be reckoned with. Yet he had sent only half out to defend the areas that had been attacked. He had not known when he gave that order either that the two enemy columns had been destroyed. It was a large enough force to defeat them, but still a small number to send. It allowed for no setbacks. For instance, if there were a third column, or some other attack being prepared.

Shar looked around her village, and she saw it in a new light. The chief had the largest hut on the highest ground, and he was the wealthiest of them all. Yet it was still a hut and nothing more. She remembered the winter two years gone where the roof blew off in a storm and all that was inside was ruined by water. For all his grand ways, he was just a villager like the rest of them, and he lived in a village where poverty ruled.

The track she trod was rutted, and pools of water lay in it. Chickens and ducks roamed freely, their droppings everywhere. Likewise, pigs rooted around in the churned earth around the huts. It was all she had ever known herself, but she knew there was better. Her grandmother had described stone buildings to her, and mansions and even palaces. She had spoken of banquets where the food thrown out afterward was better fare than they saw here on feast days.

A burning desire took hold of her. Despite all this, the Fen Wolves were a great people. They had courage and high spirit. They valued honesty and good will. She wanted to bring them out of this poverty and into triumph, and perhaps she would one day.

But for all the poverty she saw, including the dirty faces that peered out at them from inside the huts as they trod the path, this was still her home and she loved it.

Her home village might be bigger, but it was really not so different from the one she saw recently, burned and destroyed, its people murdered. Could that happen here? She knew it was so. Tension between the clans was always high, and she had little faith in the chief. He was the shaman's man, and the shamans did what was best for themselves. If they decreed the fens would fall to the Soaring Eagles, then fall it would.

The leng-fah came to the hut of the chief. There, Argash went inside to make his report. The rest of them separated, and Shar walked on toward the hut where she lived with her grandmother. She felt suddenly angry at all that had happened, and she felt a little worried too. Her words *would* be repeated to the shaman, or those who were closely allied to him. It would cause her trouble, but she did not regret them. They were the truth, and if more people voiced the truth in their hearts, then the dark force that controlled all the clans from the shadows would be more clearly seen for what it was.

She approached her hut. It was better than some, but not as good as the chief's. Yet it was home to her, and there she would find her grandmother, or at least the person who went by that title even if she was not related, and receive wise counsels and affection. In truth, she *was* her grandmother, and it did not matter that they weren't related by blood. Their ties were stronger than that.

She came to the door, and carved into the rough timber was the same sign that she had grown up seeing – a circle of herbs. It was the mark of a witch, and while they held far less power over the land than shamans, witches were common, and their knowledge of healing and minor spells much sought after by the people.

Her grandmother was more than a witch though, even if people in this village did not know it. Yet they did know that her skill at healing was great, and many were the villagers alive today who owed their lives to her.

She went inside, and her grandmother was there at the table, a welcoming smile on her face and two plates of food already set out.

"Eat first," she said, "and then we'll talk."

How had the old woman known that she was returning? But it was no surprise. She always seemed to know.

Shar went over and kissed her on the brow, then she sat.

"Eat," the old woman repeated. "You're tired, and you'll need strength soon."

Shar felt suddenly starving. She was indeed tired, but the tone of her grandmother was troubling. She knew, or guessed, at least some of what happened.

They ate in silence, for Shar was ravenous. Her grandmother ate little, but that was normal for her. She was barely more than skin and bones, and her long white hair seemed as big as her body. Yet she was still strong, stronger by far than anyone in the village knew.

When they were done, her grandmother looked up at her.

"You're in danger, child."

"I know. I was rash, and I spoke my heart. It was not wise. Not yet, anyway."

Her grandmother sat back in her chair. She seemed impossibly ancient, and Shar knew many in the village venerated her. Go Shan, they called her, which was more title than name, but even Shar called her that, and had since she could remember. Daughter of wisdom it meant, and it was a title of great respect.

"Tell me all," her grandmother said.

Shar held nothing back. She was not sure what her grandmother already knew. But past experience had taught her that the important facts were likely known, though not the details. How her grandmother did this, she did not know. It was magic, and of a kind that made the spells of the shaman seem the prattling of a child. If he knew that she was stronger by far than him, he would have felt fear such as he had never known, for despite all his pride she could kill him easier than a man kills a mosquito that lands on his neck, and with less remorse. She had no love for the shamans.

"I am proud of you, child."

Shar had expected a reprimand. "But I spoke hastily, and now I think I'll regret it."

"That may be, but as I think you'll soon learn it might have been fate that put those words in your mouth. The world is shifting, and all that was certain is uncertain. Destiny blows on the wind, and those who reach for it might be blown into the abyss or raised high. Change is

61

coming, child. I feel it in my bones, and my bones don't lie to me."

Shar was silent. Could this be the hour that she had been preparing for since childhood?

"Show me the parchment," her grandmother asked.

Shar withdrew the message she had found on the body of the Ahat, and passed it over.

Go Shan took it, but did not read it straight away. "You have trained all your life, and you are the best warrior of the Fen Wolves, and likely one of the best in the land. But to defeat an Ahat, that is something special. They are the best of the best. Be proud of that, but learn from it also. No training can substitute for how you felt and reacted when you fought him. Analyze it. Learn from it. One such fight to the death is worth a decade of sparring sessions."

"I will, grandmother."

The old woman looked at the paper then, and her face was still as a stone and betrayed no emotion. By that stillness Shar knew that Go Shan could not only read the message but that it was bad news.

A long time the old woman held the paper, then as though coming out of a sleep she started to move once more. She drew her plate closer, and in her hand the message blossomed into fire.

Her grandmother was careful with her use of magic. She seldom practiced it in the village where the shaman might sense her. More often, especially when using the higher magics to teach Shar the arts of fighting, they would walk into a lonely spot of the fen. There she would summon her shade-warriors, beings that seemed of flesh and blood yet were nothing but magic, and there Shar would spar them, honing her skills in ways that few other warriors ever had.

Only when the flame reached Go Shan's fingertips did she drop what remained of the paper onto her plate. There it burned to a layer of ash, and even those ashes she disturbed with her finger to work complete destruction.

"I could not read it, grandmother. What did it say?"

Shar thought at first that her grandmother had not heard her, but then she stirred in her chair.

"It was written in an old tongue, one which the shamans used since before the Shadowed Wars. It is one which only they know, and few others of wisdom that were in the court of the emperor." The old lady sighed, and her gaze fell again to the ashes.

"What did it say?" Shar repeated.

"I fear we are discovered, child. It said *One thousand gold pieces to whomever finds nuhar.*"

Shar frowned. "It's not much of a message. And who is Nuhar?"

Go Shan rubbed her temples. "Nuhar isn't a person, but a term. It means *the hunted one.*"

That sent a shiver up Shar's spine. "Then they have discovered I'm descended of the emperor?"

"They have." The old woman paused then. "Though it might refer to me as well. The shamans have searched for me since the time of your great forefather."

Shar had heard all the stories since she was old enough to be trusted to keep the secret. Her grandmother was not her grandmother, but the great shaman Shulu Gan, she who defied the shamans and had been cast from their order. She that had forged the twin swords of the emperor to protect him from their sorcery. And she that legend claimed raised the descendants of the emperor in secret. The shamans hated her, and even after all these years they wanted to kill her. But most of all, they wanted the secret of the magic in the swords. For while those blades endured, then the prophesy went that a descendent of the emperor would rise up to challenge them.

"It doesn't really matter who they hunt," the old lady continued. "If it's you they'll find me, and if it's me they'll find you. Certainly, there's no one else in Tsarin Fen for whom an Ahat would be sent."

Shar took a deep breath. "Then is the moment here? Will I be the descendant, of all the generations you have guarded, to fulfil the prophecy?"

The old woman reached out and placed her hands on top of Shar's where they rested on the table.

"You are yourself first, before anything else. Remember that. Remember it always. Will you fulfil the prophecy? I cannot say. The time draws near, that much I feel. You will be tested shortly. Your life hangs upon a thread. I can say no more. I know no more. But whatever fate throws at you, look it bravely in the eyes. *That*, I know you will do."

Shar could never quite tell when her grandmother was holding back information. She thought that was the case now, but she could not be sure. Nor did it matter. If she did, there was a purpose to it, and the trust between them was complete. Time would prove her right for doing so.

"Then what now?" Shar asked.

"For now, we wait. Soon a knock will come at the door. You'll go to the chief, and it will not be good news. After that, we'll be forced our separate ways. It's no longer safe here for either of us."

Shar held back her tears. "Will we meet again in this world?"

"I am old Shar, very old. I am ancient beyond ancient, but I know the magic that the sages of the east learned long ago. It has kept me alive, but not for much longer. My time is growing close. Yet know this! We will meet again, and though you will not realize it, I will be closer to you than you think. Always. In the meantime, others will take my place."

Shar bowed her head, but said nothing. She could find no words.

"Be at peace, child," Go Shan continued. "This is the way of things, and all who live must endure partings. But you are strong! I will take up yet another disguise as I have through the ages, and for you it is time to go out into the world. There you will meet friends and foes and fate. You will be equal to them all. Know also that even as your great forefather would be proud of you, so too am I. You go with my love."

Shar got out of her chair and hugged the old woman fiercely.

"I love you, Shulu," she whispered. Her grandmother's real name was rarely ever spoken, but on special occasions she used it.

The old lady hugged her back, and there was strength in her arms that none would suspect. Yet even as they embraced a knock came at the door.

"Go now, as you must, Shar," the old woman whispered in her ear. "Fate moves apace, and destiny calls. The blood of your forefather calls. But I promise, we *will* meet again."

Shar did not want to let go of the old woman, still less leave. It had to be done though, so she walked over to the door and opened it.

"The chief wants to see you," said the young man there. He was a grandson of the chief, and he smirked at her. He knew some of what was coming.

Shar did not answer. Instead, she looked back at her grandmother and gave a wave. All words that needed saying had been.

She closed the door and followed the young man toward the chief's hut. Her heart was grown suddenly cold, and she fingered the hilt of her sword. She would be rebuked, that much was certain. Yet the chief, and the shaman who would be there as well, had best not push her too far.

A horn began to blow. It was the one used to summon the whole village to hear the chief or shaman speak. To Shar, it seemed to summon something else. A new life beckoned.

She walked in silence, and the young man with her said nothing, but the smirk never left his face. Perhaps, one day when he was older, he would have a better appreciation of how the world worked and that he served a cause that pulled humanity down rather than lifted it up.

Not once did Shar look back to the hut where she and her grandmother lived. If she did, she might cry for she knew that the person she loved most in the world was gathering together what was needful to her and fleeing the swamp while the rest of the community gathered to hear the chief.

Shar wished that she had said more to her, and thanked her for all she had done, and told her again that she loved her. She felt guilty that she had not said enough, but sometimes she found it hard to say these things, and she wondered if all her training since early childhood had made her more like a man than a girl.

They came to the open space before the chief's hut. There was already a large crowd there, but more were gathering.

The chief did not wait for everyone. He stepped forward, holding high his staff of office, and the shaman mirrored him, making eldritch signs with his hands. The villagers believed he made incantations when he did so, but Go Shan had only grinned at that idea and told her privately that the man barely possessed any magic at all, and that the gestures were mere show to fool the superstitious.

Shar did not like the man. He gave her the creeps, and he had openly mocked her grandmother calling her a poor witch of little strength. She had merely shrugged, and he had been unwitting that he was in the presence of a power greater by far than his than the sun is at noon compared to the light of the stars through a clouded sky. She could have struck him down with fire and burned him to ash, and he did not know.

But the shaman was not one of the long-lived. Only their elite understood the magic of longevity. He could not recognize her, for he had not known her of old. Other shamans might, but she had changed herself in many ways, and grown her hair long which now had turned silver. She did not think that any could.

Shar's thoughts were broken by the chief beginning to speak.

"We have been attacked," the man said, going on to explain events as Argash would have reported them. He did not seem overly concerned. Maybe that was because he had not seen the smoke rise from a destroyed village like Shar had. Or maybe he thought he was safe in the heart of the fen, and he did not care that much about people he ruled but rarely met.

When the chief was done, the shaman began to speak. Shar was still waiting for her rebuke, and if the chief did not give it to her, then the shaman would.

The shaman was an old man, and he was overweight and white haired. The latter was common enough in Tsarin Fen, but in a land of poverty where many children died from malnutrition, the first was rare.

"I have other news than the chief," he said. While he spoke, his gaze rested on Shar for a moment, and she felt malevolence there. Her words had been reported back, that much was certain. But he did not mention her, at least yet.

"You all know that this is a triseptium year. Three times seven years the shamans of old went into exile of some kind or another before they managed to bring order to the wide lands of the Cheng. And to celebrate that, every twenty-one years we hold the Quest of Swords. I can announce what you did not know before. This time, the quest will be held in spring. It starts today!"

Shar looked around. She did not think the people were ready for this yet. Even if the chief did not seem worried by enemy attacks, they were. Yet among the warriors she saw an air of excitement. Some of them, especially the younger ones like herself, knew this was an opportunity to change their lives forever. For them, they hoped to find the swords, and they hoped, if secretly, that they were descended of the old emperor. But mostly, they knew the shamans followed all news of those who went on the quest, and that if they proved themselves as they traveled across a dangerous land, then they would be offered wealth and training to become *nazram*, the elite warriors who served the shamans themselves.

It was different for her. She cared nothing for the prestige and wealth of being a nazram. She *was* descended from the emperor, and if she fulfilled his dying prophecy then she would bring freedom to all the lands of the Cheng and glory to the Fen Wolves.

The shaman was not done. He turned his gaze back to Shar, and she saw the malevolence brighten in his eyes. Raising his arm and pointing at her with one fat finger, he spoke in an angry tone.

"The one among us called Shar has let the tribe down. Argash tells me she showed courage in the battle, but that is of no account to me. What use is courage if the mind that goes with it is twisted?"

Shar felt the eyes of the village upon her. She stood a little taller and looked boldly back at the shaman. Whatever was said she would show no hurt.

"This woman has dared to criticize the shamans. After all that we have done for the nation, she harbors ill will against us. That will not be tolerated. If I had the power, I would ban her from going on the Quest of Swords, for she is a warrior who is proud of her prowess and will no doubt seek advancement from it. Alas, I do not have that power, for the right of all to go on that quest has come down from of old, and has not been changed. Not yet, anyway."

Here the shaman raised his voice and spoke as though pronouncing a judgement, even though only the chiefs could do so.

"But I have this power, and I use it. I forbid any of you to serve as her witnesses during the quest. It is a requirement that any quester takes two witnesses with them who do not desire to be nazram themselves but who can testify before a shaman as to the quester's deeds. Let none of you aid her, or my wrath will fall upon you! I have spoken."

The shaman stepped back then, and he looked satisfied with himself. But Shar nearly laughed. The man was a fat, pompous fool. Those rules were the edicts of the shamans, and they had nothing to do with her forefather's prophecy.

"I care less than nothing for becoming a nazram," she replied in a cool voice. "I care only for my people, which is all the Cheng tribes. Too long have we suffered under the yoke of the shamans. They say they bring peace, but they give us only war. They claim to nurture prosperity, but look around! The give us poverty instead. I hope the swords are found, and I hope the descendent of the emperor wields them well!"

It was a bold thing to say. Perhaps even stupid, for the shamans held all the power in the land. Yet she was far from alone in thinking it, and even though she had invited their wrath, it was worth it. Change was in the air, for good or ill, and she would cast her life into the currents of fate and see where they swept her. If the shamans were to be overthrown, the roaring blaze that would do it must start with a spark. And she would cast it now. Her words were bold, and the example of them would spread wide.

Before the shaman or the chief could reply, she turned her back on them and walked away. Everything she had done was an insult and a challenge to their authority, and she felt suddenly free of shackles that had bound her all her life. But there would be consequences…

8. A Strange Meeting

Asana came to the ridge, and looked out at the vision below.

He was high up amid the mountains and he loved it here. Or he would have except that he and his companion had been forced by rumors of bandits to travel closer to Three Moon Mountain than he liked. He glanced at it in turn, towering above him to the right. It was snow-capped and beautiful, but Kubodin must have sensed his thoughts.

"Evil ever puts on a fair cloak," he said.

Asana glanced at his friend in turn. Kubodin looked a vagabond with his brass earring and rope belt holding together clothes that most farmers would think too dirty to clean a pigsty in. But his mind was sharp as a razor-edged sword.

"So it does. Do the shamans think themselves evil, though?"

"Most folks that are don't think of themselves as such. But deep down they know if they let their thoughts delve that far."

That was certainly true. No doubt the shamans had chosen the beauty of that mountain to hide their fortress. Like an apple eaten out inside by worms that mountain was said to be tunneled deep and far by them. What they did there, few knew. Yet their sorcery was always dark.

Asana looked ahead again. The sooner they left this place the better. He did not like being in sight of those he hated. Likewise, the shamans were not friendly to him.

Ahead, he saw the wide expanse of his homeland. The mountains seemed to tumble down into the faraway plains, for there were long lines of hills and slopes of scree. The plains in turn dropped lower in places, and he saw the dark smudge of Tsarin Fen. He had never been there, but he and Kubodin would go past it on their journey.

"It seems a good day to travel," Kubodin commented, squinting up into the clear sky.

Asana agreed, yet they had been forced to abandon their journey only yesterday, which had started much the same way, and seek shelter when a late spring blizzard made it hard to find the path and caused the temperature to plummet. They had been lucky to find a cave. That luck might not hold up again, but at least they were heading downhill now and the danger to them would diminish quickly.

He glanced once more at Three Moon Mountain, and then stepped briskly ahead. Kubodin shuffled along beside him, his hand never too far from the axe thrust through his rope belt.

The walking was easy, being downhill, and they set a good pace. There were few trees up this high, but ahead was a patch. It would help hide them, which Asana liked for he did not feel comfortable being in the open. He trusted his sword skills, and Kubodin with his axe, to deal with any threat. Except one that the shamans might pose. He had seen his fill of sorcery in the past, and he did not like it.

The path was clear, and the day was bright. The sky seemed impossibly blue and the air fresh enough to make breathing seem like drinking wine. Yet he slowed, and that sense that warned him of danger flared.

Kubodin felt it too. "Do you think there are people in that stand of trees?"

"I don't know. Something is wrong here though."

Kubodin tugged on his earring. "Be that as it may, this path is the only safe way down the mountain, and I'm not turning back. So let's go forward a little and see what we can discover."

Neither of them drew their weapons. That might send the wrong signal if there was someone friendly ahead. Yet friendly people were few and far between in the wild lands.

Overhead, two eagles wheeled in slow circles, rising higher into the clear sky. From somewhere far below them on the slope a flock of rock pigeons landed in a flurry of wings on a ledge sheltered by a towering cliff. Asana saw all these things, and he noted them, for observation was the key to staying alive in a wild land where predators, on two feet or four, might otherwise creep up on a traveler by surprise. Yet he kept most of his attention on the patch of woodland before them.

"There's something in the shadow of the wood lying over the track," he said.

Kubodin grunted. "I see it."

They slowed their pace, yet still they drew no weapons.

"Come to me," came a voice, and it seemed to drift to them from all around rather than the one spot.

They gave no answer, but they walked within twenty feet of the shadow and there they paused. Still, they could not see what was there, for the shadows moved in a dappled light from the wood. Here, they drew their weapons, for they were close enough to the wood itself that they might be rushed by any who lay in wait.

The voice sounded again, and there was a note of amusement in it. It was a woman's voice, and it had something of the tone of a mother gently scolding a child.

"Don't wave that axe at me, Kubodin. Have you no manners?"

"It's *my* axe, and I'll wave it where I like."

"Is it?" replied the voice. "I suppose it is. At least, you own it for now. But it was *I* who made it long ago, and there is that within it that will not harm me. That is how the magic of such things works. What craftsperson would make a weapon that could be used against them?"

Kubodin gave no answer to that, but the mention of magic in the axe unnerved Asana. There *was* magic in his friend's axe, but who would know such a thing?

"Come to me," the voice said again, and this time it held a note of command.

"You come to *us*," Asana replied. "Show yourself."

There was a silence. Then the voice came again, and it was serious now. The humor was gone. Even the command was gone. This was a voice that *expected* obedience as though the owner were a queen. "Come," it asked, and despite himself, Asana took another step forward, then paused. He was about to ask once more for whoever it was to show themselves, for now he knew beyond doubt that magic was being used. He could see the pool of shadows well enough to know that no person could be hiding in them, yet that was where the voice was coming from.

The shadows moved, and then suddenly he saw a figure. It was not a real person, but a thing of shadow and dappled light, yet as it stepped closer its form was perfectly clear. It was a woman. An old, old woman. She was slight and frail, and her long hair was silver as moonlight.

The figure only took a few paces, and then stopped. "I want no eyes to see me save your own, and this is a land where there are many watchful gazes. Even the eagles that circle in the sky can serve as the windows for others."

Asana knew who she meant. He had not realized it before, but perhaps by sorcery the shamans could know all that passed in their land. Or through it. It was not a pleasant realization.

Kubodin tugged at his earring again. It was always a gesture of thoughtfulness, and then he dropped his hand quickly and even lowered his axe, but not all the way.

"There are legends in my family, lady. I think I know who you are."

She grinned at him. "I know who you are, Kubodin, and the long line of your ancestors back to one who sat at the emperor's side and gave him counsels. And when courage was called for, he rode beside him in battle too. He was much like you, and because I liked him, and because Chen Fei liked him, I crafted that very axe that you now wield."

Kubodin began to tremble, and he went down on one knee.

"Thank you, Great Lady. That was the legend in my family, and we have always been proud of it. But until today I didn't know if it was true. Now I do, and it pleases me."

Asana had never seen his friend like this before, and he could not understand what was happening. There was a sheen of tears in Kubodin's eyes, and the hand that held the axe trembled.

The old lady laughed, and suddenly she seemed different. She was small and frail, but Asana sensed that she was like a vessel. However frail she seemed, that was only the outside shell. Inside, she was a creature of raw power.

"Tell your friend, the swordmaster Asana, who I am," she commanded.

Kubodin did not hesitate. He did not even question how she knew both their names.

"This is Taga Nashu. The Grandmother Who Does Not Die, as legend calls her. But she has other names. One of them you may have heard before. Shulu Gan."

Asana could not believe it, but it all made sense now. He felt her power, and he sensed the truth of things. Even as Kubodin had, he went down on one knee. It was a salute of great respect, yet even so he still distrusted magic, and the legends of her said that she could be capricious and violent. He saluted, but he did not lower the tip of his sword.

Shulu Gan looked at them mysteriously. "I have need of you. Will you serve the empire that was, and could yet be?"

Asana had little love for the shamans. But this would be dangerous. Perhaps more dangerous than anything he had done before, and his life had not been without risk. Yet still, he did not wish to refuse her.

Kubodin grinned. "Whatever you ask must carry great danger. Otherwise you would not ask in secret. Yet the legends say you are generous to those who help you. Is that so?"

The old lady laughed. "To help me is to help yourself. Do you not return to the hills where you were born? Has not your brother usurped the chieftainship of your clan, and do you not journey there to right that wrong and help your people?"

"I do, lady."

"Then know this. You journey to your death, and Asana, because he is your friend, will die with you. Yet I can prevent that and help you regain what was stolen from you. So you will both benefit from aiding me."

Kubodin shrugged. "All of us die sooner or later. Though perhaps not you."

She looked at him sternly now. "You have given yourself time to think, which is all you really want with this pretense at bartering. But my time runs short, and you must make your choice swiftly. Will you help me?"

76

Kubodin stood up, and Asana did likewise. "We will," they both said in unison. There had never been any doubt in Asana's mind, but he never liked agreeing to things too quickly.

"What must we do?" he asked.

"Something that will seem likely to get you killed. Yet, on my word, you have more chance of surviving than if you go on your way without helping me."

9. The Old Blood

Asana felt at peace. He was a swordmaster of unparalleled skill. What was the use of that if he could not serve a needful cause? Life was not worth living if you hid away in fear and never took risks.

All that remained for him to know was what that cause was. If it was good, any risk was worth taking. Even so, he mistrusted magic, and he knew that whatever Shulu Gan wanted the shamans would try to stop.

"Let us speak plainly," he said. "Neither I nor Kubodin are friends of the shamans, and had we lived at the time we would have supported the emperor. But you know this already else you would not have approached us. So, what do you wish of us? I do not speak for Kubodin, but I will not give aid to a cause I don't believe in."

Shulu Gan bowed. She was a thing of shadow and dappled light, yet she seemed impossibly frail and looked like a sparrow pecking at the ground. If this sending looked like her real body, and he believed that it did, she must be close to death.

"You speak well and truly, and with more foresight than you know. I don't expect blind obedience, and in fact it annoys me. You said you would have served the emperor? Well, that can never be. He is murdered, and the memory of that day has haunted me through the long centuries. But even though he is dead, the legends of what happened after are true."

Asana heard Kubodin hiss between his teeth. The man was surprised, which he rarely was. And no wonder.

"The legend," Asana said quietly, "is that you saved a descendant of the emperor. It is said that you have hidden his descendants through all these years, and that one day the prophecy of the emperor himself will be fulfilled. One of his blood will rise to challenge the shamans."

Shulu Gan gazed at them both in turn, and whatever the frailty of her body Asana sensed the shear, implacable determination of her will.

"I will say openly to the two of you what none save myself and one other in all the land know for certain. That legend is true. A descendant of the emperor lives. The generations have been many, but the old blood still runs in the veins of one worthy to help the Cheng nation and bring the shamans to their knees. The time of the prophecy is come, and the world will tremble."

Asana felt a thrill run through him. It was one thing to guess, but another thing to know.

Shulu Gan stepped closer. "Her name is Shar, and she needs your help. She is the destiny of this land, and if she dies then the future of this land dies with her. So, I ask again, will you help?"

Asana felt a sense of awe. "I will," he whispered. "I pledge it on my life."

"And you, Kubodin?"

The little man gave a curt nod. "I pledge on my life also."

Shulu Gan seemed pleased. "Shar is in great danger. It may be that our secret is discovered, though I do not know how. But no secret lasts forever. Yet either her or I are hunted by the Ahat. Her chief, and the shaman of her tribe are also enemies to her. And for all that she may become in the future she is still just a young woman. She will go on the Quest of Swords, which has just been announced, and it will seem that all the world is against her."

"Is that what we are to do?" Asana asked. "Help her find the swords?"

Shulu Gan shook her head. "It may be that you will help her with that. I cannot see the paths of the future as once I did. Your first task is just to help her stay alive."

"If sword and axe can serve," Kubodin said, "we'll do our bit. Where is she?"

Shulu Gan seemed to flicker as though a cloud passed over the sun.

"I grow weak," she muttered. "Just when I need my greatest strength. No matter, though. Time defeats us all, one day. As for where she is, it's not important. Your destiny is linked to hers. Fate will guide your footsteps. Just head down the mountain and you will be sure to find her."

This was exactly the sort of thing that Asana disliked. It was all vague, and it reeked of magic.

"How will we know her when we meet her?"

Shulu Gan laughed. "Oh, you'll know her. Don't worry about that. The greater problem is this. She doesn't know that I'm sending help. She won't trust you, or even agree to let you accompany her. But I have something that will help with that."

The ancient shaman delved beneath her cloak, and then she drew out a small object and handed it to Asana.

"She will recognize this," the old woman said. "She has seen it in our hut since she was a child."

Asana looked at what he had been given. It seemed real enough, although he was sure that the shaman's hand had touched his and he had felt nothing. But the object was different. It was small enough to fit in his palm, and it was heavy for its size. It was a statue of baked clay, and looking closely at it he marveled at the craft that produced it. The thing was a precise replica of the shaman herself. Her slight frame, the hard and intelligent look in her eyes, and the long silver hair were all perfect. Even the clothes that decorated it were the same as what she wore now.

"It's a marvelous piece of artistry," he said.

Her eyes gleamed at that. "Better even than you know. Do not lose it or cast it away. Ever. Keep it with you at all times, even after you've proved to Shar that I sent you. I want it back one day when all this is over."

Again, Asana felt that magic was involved. Perhaps it was a talisman of some kind that offered protection against the magic of the shamans.

The figure of Shulu Gan wavered once more, and this time Asana saw strain on her face. She raised a hand to reach out toward them both. It might have been a gesture of blessing, or perhaps she wanted to say more. Whatever it meant, he had no chance to find out more. The figure simply faded away until all that was left was the wavering of her silver hair, and then that was gone too.

There was a deep silence, then Kubodin grunted. "Fate will guide our footsteps? Pah! Pigs will grow horns and turn into unicorns more likely. I don't believe it. We're working to her plan, and she knows more than she told us."

Asana grinned and patted his friend on the back with gusto. "Never were truer words spoken. Still, were you ever going to say no?"

"No. Of course not. Still, it feels like we're being used."

"I think so too. Even so, I wouldn't say no either. And we may benefit from this as she says."

Kubodin ran the handle of his axe through his belt, and then pulled his trousers a little higher. The axe always weighed them down. "If we live through it," he answered.

"True words," Asana agreed. "Anyway, what do you think this Shar person is like?"

Kubodin shrugged, and began to walk down the track once more. "Only one way to find out."

They continued ahead. Soon they had left the patch of trees and walked once more in the open. High above the eagles still soared, but the currents of air on which they rode seemed now to take them back up toward the peaks of the mountain.

10. The Quest Begins

Shar walked out into the fen. After what she had said to the shaman, she did not think she would be safe returning to the hut. Yet the real reason was that she could not face going there alone. Her grandmother would have left it by now, and she could not face the grief of being there by herself with only her memories for company.

It was better to be out and doing. Traveling the swamp always seemed to calm her mind anyway. It was like a wise friend that could give companionship without speech. It made her feel at home.

She began to order her mind. The Quest of Swords had begun. She knew it would be this year, though no one knew when. Her grandmother though … she had said nothing, but she must have known. She did have moments of foretelling, but in this case it was likely one of her spies that had informed her. There were many of these, mostly those that her grandmother had healed and saved from death. Probably one of them had heard the shaman speaking to the chief.

The quest was something that she thought of often. It was her chance to become the heir to her great forefather that the land needed. Yet how many other descendants of the emperor, her antecedents in turn, had lived and dreamed of doing so as well, but to no avail? How many had gone on the quest and failed? How many had her grandmother helped raise a family, and then buried in the course of the years?

Her grandmother was strong to do that. To live that long with the shadow of grief over all that she saw. Few could do that and not bow under the weight of sorrow.

It was no good thinking like this though. If she were to give herself the best chance of succeeding at the quest she must concentrate on that alone, and go through what was needed step by step.

Food was the first issue. She had little left of what she had taken on patrol, and she did not want to return to the hut. That could be resolved though. She set her steps on a path toward a place she knew. It was close, and hidden in the top of a tree was a stash of dried food. She and her grandmother kept several such stashes all through the fen in case of emergency. Such was life when the shamans would have you killed on sight if they discovered who you were.

The path she took led her into a lower part of the fen. Open bodies of stagnant water lay everywhere, and the smell of swamp gas was strong. She found the trail she was looking for. It was a muddy path that wound between two bodies of water.

The smell of the swamp gas was nearly overwhelming. It was in places such as these, where few people ventured, that the stashes were hidden.

There was a movement on the ground to her left, and she caught the undulations in the grass there that signified the passage of a snake. There were many in the fens, and some of them were deadly. It was impossible to say what variety this was, so she stamped her foot several times to make sure it knew she was there. Snakes generally dispersed when a human came along, but a few types were aggressive. Seeing no further sign of it, she continued slowly ahead.

It was not long before she found what she sought. There was a small stand of the shabby oak trees that grew in the fen, but the one she was looking for was just as she remembered it. The trunk had been struck by lightning years ago, and it also leaned away from the others at an angle.

Shar looked around. There was no sign of anyone nearby. Quickly she began to climb the trunk, using her feet and hands together in an awkward clamber that did not look pretty but that got her into the canopy quickly. There she found the bag she was looking for. It was filled with nuts and the hard, dry biscuits made of flour, seeds, honey and special herbs to help preserve it. She did not like the taste of them, but they served their purpose.

She dropped down quickly, checked the contents to make sure all was well, and then went on her way. There were several coins there as well. Enough to help her for some of her journey. For the rest, she would have to rely on luck.

Sweat trickled down her back, and the flies annoyed her. She headed south now, not knowing why but picking a direction at random. Her next step was to leave the swamp, but what then?

She had no idea where the swords were hidden. She knew the story from her grandmother of how they had been taken by the shamans. But most people knew that legend. What she did not know was where they had been taken to. Asking her grandmother had not helped. Shulu had merely shrugged on those frequent occasions and said she did not know. The shamans would have hidden them somewhere dangerous though, which could be just about anywhere.

One thing her grandmother was sure of was that the swords still existed. She always smiled mysteriously at that, and said her magic was higher, if more dangerous, than that of her enemies. The swords could not be destroyed, and they were out there somewhere, waiting through the long years for the right person to wield them. It was a strange way to talk about swords too, as though they were alive and could wait, but her grandmother, for all that Shar loved her, could be strange at times.

She pushed on, for the day was passing and she wished to be far from the village as soon as possible. She avoided all other villages too. All she wanted was to be alone and to sort through all the different feelings she had.

At times, she saw other travelers in the fen. They, like her, were heading outward. She took them for other hunters of the swords, for they journeyed in parties of three. Most likely they were a quester and the two witnesses. She gave them all a wide berth. Likewise, they avoided her.

The long shadows of afternoon fell over the swamp. It was dangerous to travel at night, for it was hard to gauge direction and the chances of a misstep were greater. Not to mention the risks of falling foul of some night-crawling snake or other creature.

She headed for high ground and made camp on a small rise. It was grown over with stunted oaks, some of which had fallen in ages past and begun to rot. Yet there was one recent treefall, and the timber seemed dry. Of this, she collected enough wood to light a fire, and to keep it going through the night. That would warn away most prowling creatures, and the smoke would repel mosquitoes.

Dawn saw her moving on once more, just another shadow in the fens slipping silently along the secret paths. The sun was well up, and she was close to the border of her homeland, before she stopped for a rest and half a biscuit.

She finished her meagre meal, and then stood to continue on when she noticed something wrong. At first, she was not sure what it was. Then she knew. Her backtrail was quiet. No sound came from that direction, and it spoke of a large group of people moving quickly rather than a single traveler or group of three. This was her home, and she had nothing to fear here. Yet she had not liked the look in the shaman's eye, and a sense of foreboding touched her.

11. Hunted

Shar made a quick decision. It was better to be safe than sorry, and she looked around for a place to hide. Moving off the path she angled toward a clump of bushes and hunkered down inside their thick cover.

A long time seemed to pass, and she saw nothing. She began to wonder if she had let anxiety get the better of her when she saw a man emerge on the track that she herself had walked some while ago. But it was not just one man.

Soon she saw a group of a half dozen men. These were not questers for the swords, nor members of a leng-fah patrol. They were warriors, and they looked alert.

She eased herself deeper into the bushes and waited. They were not likely to find her, if they were searching for her at all. And she had been careful to leave the track where there was solid ground and where she had left little trail.

The men came closer. They walked in single file, and they kept a keen eye on all around them. Yet the one who was leading them slowed from time to time and studied the trail. Shar cursed silently, for he had the look of a tracker about him. Her cursing grew more strident in her mind when she recognized some of the men. They were nazram warriors, serving only the shaman.

Fear crept up on her. She could think of no reason for the men to be here. They served only the shaman and never went on patrols. They were good swordsmen all, and most were not even of the Fen Wolf Tribe. So it was with the nazram. Once a warrior served the shamans they could move freely about the land and often did, moving from one shaman to another.

Shar studied them closely. They were near enough now to see their expressions, and they looked grim. It was another bad sign. Yet if the worst should happen, despite them being good warriors and outnumbering her, she had one advantage. She was much younger, for most of these men had risen to the order of nazram twenty-one years ago, and were probably about that age at the time.

They drew nearly level with her, and the man in the lead slowed, and then dropped to his haunches. He studied the ground intently, then he rose, took several paces in her direction, and then suddenly raised his arm and pointed.

"She's close!" the man said. Quickly, the rest of them drew their blades. There was no mistaking their intention now, and Shar swore to herself that one day she would bring the shamans down. If she lived.

There was only one thing to do. If she stayed where she was, they would find her. She crawled backward, found a way out of the bushes and set off at an easy lope.

Immediately, the call went up that she had been seen, and the chase commenced. There was nothing for it but this. There was not enough cover to think about trying to escape without being seen. But this way, she had a head start, and she was younger and fitter. At least, she hoped so.

She pushed ahead, finding a path wherever she went, for she knew this part of the fen well. The nazram would not. They did not go out on patrols, and mostly they lazed around the shaman's hut playing dice or, less often, sparring with swords or fists. If she could get ahead of them she might have a chance to slip away.

Against that was the tracker. He would not be fooled, and she would not have enough time to try to hide her trail properly.

They were gaining on her. She heard their rush through the fen. The sound of bodies brushing against leaves and branches came to her, and louder and louder the heavy stamp of boots. Sometimes there were curses as they left the trail and stepped in boggy earth that she had avoided. Yet they *were* gaining on her, and she felt the stab of fear and an overwhelming urge to run faster.

She stifled that urge. Over a short distance she could never outrun them. Yet if she managed to keep ahead for a little while, and not to overexert herself, then she was sure she could endure longer than they could, and eventually increase her lead.

A spear flew past her head. She paid little heed to it. Spears and bows were uncommon in the fen. There would probably be no more, but she wished she had observed them more closely to check their weapons before she broke from cover.

She ran on, and then veered suddenly to the left and went down a slippery slope of a gulley. She tripped and fell, then came to her feet and raced on. Ahead was one of the many corrugated paths of logs that made travel through the fens easier. But this was an old one, and the logs were rotted.

Slowing her pace as much as she dared, she chose her path carefully across it. The group of nazram came up behind her, but she had an advantage here. She weighed less, and she knew how dangerous this particular path was. Her pursuers had probably never been here.

Another spear crashed into the trees to her right, and she cursed for she knew the enemy was very close now. Yet even as she did so there was a scream from behind her. She looked back. One of the men was down, and he looked in a bad way. A rotted log had given way beneath him and his foot had fallen through. He had fallen, and likely broken his leg. At least she hoped so.

The others kept coming though, leaving their companion to scream and struggle by himself. She dared not look back again, but raced forward as fast as she thought possible. If she fell like her pursuer had, it would be all over for her. Yet she was light, and the fear of death was upon her. She glided forward like the fen wolf she admired so much, swift of pace and sure of footing.

Her enemy fell back. She did not take the time to look, but she heard from the sounds of pursuit that they had slowed. It was no great surprise. They were not in fear of their lives as she was, and she used that to her advantage.

The path of logs dipped low, turned to the right and then began to ascend. She knew this place, and what lay beyond. She thought as she ran, for a choice lay before her. Suddenly, the log trail ceased, and then she climbed a slight hill. The enemy were behind her, still taking their time on the logs, and she dashed ahead.

The rise did not last long. Soon, the track sloped downhill again, but there were no more logs. The trail itself was firm, and the trees thinned out. Ahead was a long stretch of low land, much of it covered by grass. There were plenty of small stands of trees though that would offer cover. And there were bodies of water too, some of them deep.

She could keep running, and perhaps escape. But the nazram were more dogged in their pursuit than she had anticipated. An alternative was to try to hide, but she had little time for that.

Trusting to her luck, as she often did, she veered off the trail. Here, the grass was short and the narrow track firm. She would leave no sign of her passing.

With a quick sprint she covered twenty or so yards, then slipped into a stand of sedge grass. She was careful to leave little trail here as well, but the grass was thick and tall. Yet it sprang back in place after her passing and she did not think there was any sign that she had come through it. She began to crawl now, and came to one of the many pools of water that she knew dotted this area. Unlike most of the fen, these pools were deep and of clearer water. Lilies grew up through them.

She turned and waited. In only a moment her pursuers, just five strong now, raced over the slight crest and down into the lower lands. Shar watched them and breathed as deeply as she could trying to stop the heaving of her chest. If she made too much noise they might not need to see her to find her.

They raced past the point where she had hidden, and then they slowed and came to a standstill. No doubt they were confused. She might have outpaced them and hidden somewhere ahead. Or she might be close. Or she might have veered away to the side somewhere and kept going. They could not be sure which might apply.

Indecision caught them in its snare, and they came together to talk. She could not hear most of what they said, but there were many arm gestures and they seemed angry. It was well known that the shaman could be a vindictive man, and no doubt they feared to return to him and report failure in their mission.

Soon the tracker began scouting the grass while the others waited. He went back and forth, but he seemed to find nothing. This only upset them more, and after another round of heated words they split up and commenced searching in all directions, slowly quartering the area wherever the ground was firm enough.

Shar felt a stab of fear again. It seemed they did not believe that she had eluded them, but that she was somewhere close by and hiding. Given that this was true, they would discover her soon enough and the situation would be as it was earlier.

But her breathing had returned to normal now, and she had a plan that might yet fool them. Slowly she slipped back through the sedge grass and into the water. She did not want to do this, but necessity demanded it. She went in deep until just her head was above water, and half swam and half crawled to remove herself from the edge of the pool.

The water was not so deep that she could not stand with her head above it, but it did come up to her shoulders. The food that she had gone to so much trouble to retrieve would be spoiled, and there were no more stashes between here and the border of the fen. But it was better to go hungry than to die. She, like everyone who lived in the swamp lands, had endured hunger before.

She waited as long as she dared, then withdrew the reed pipe that she had taken from the Ahat who had tried to kill her. She hoped she had better luck at hiding than he had.

Even as she did so she heard a noise in the grass not so far away, and she put the pipe to her lips and submerged her head beneath the water. She was careful to make no splashing sound, or to disturb the surface of the pool and create ripples.

Breathing was harder than she thought, and she tried to slow her breath and calm herself as much as possible. With luck, the water would hide her, and so too the lilies growing up through it. Nor was it likely that anyone would pay attention to the small bit of reed sticking up.

She opened her eyes beneath the water, but she could not see anything clearly. So she closed them again, offered up a prayer to the universe to keep her safe, and waited.

All the while she feared the stab of a spear, but nothing happened.

She waited what seemed forever. At last, tired of hiding beneath the water and frustrated, she slowly lifted her head and peered out from a cluster of lilies. She saw nothing. Nor did she hear anything. Again, she waited. She was ready to submerge herself once more if the enemy came into sight, but they did not. At length, a group of ducks flew overhead, circled, and landed in another pool some distance away.

The enemy were gone. Their search had moved elsewhere, probably farther down the trail she had been following. They would not pick up her tracks there though, and that would send them back here again. It was better that she left now, if only she could be absolutely positive they really had gone.

Her time was running out, and she knew it. Better to trust to her luck again than wait and get found in a more thorough search.

She crossed noiselessly to the other side of the pool. Once there, she slipped up onto the bank and waited a few moments, watching everywhere while the water dripped from her. Then she eased herself into another clump of sedges. Slowly, clump by clump, she wound her way out of the wetland and onto higher ground.

Ahead was a small forest of the dark and shabby oaks that grew in so many areas of the fen. It offered firmer ground and swift travel. Yet it might also harbor the enemy if her guess as to their actions was wrong.

But she had no choice. She drew her sword, cursed the water that had gotten on the blade and made the handle slippery, and set off at a loping pace into the wood.

If the nazram were there, she would fight them this time. If not, and she dearly hoped not, then she would make up some time and give herself the best chance of escape. Yet even if they were not here now, that tracker would surely find her trail eventually. And then they would come after her again.

12. Clan Against Clan

It was dark amid the trees, but Shar loped along the trail at a good pace. There was smoke in the air, and she knew a village was not far away. Her grandmother had brought her here several times, for she traveled widely through the fen as a healer.

It had seemed strange at first while Shar was learning from her that the old woman could teach her some of the secrets of fighting, such as dar shun, yet that same knowledge could also be used to help heal the bodies of the sick, or to relieve them for a while of the symptoms of their illness. But then she realized that the different arts of killing and healing were just two sides of the one coin, and the better you understood how to do one the better you understood how to do the other.

She turned away from the village. She did not want to meet anyone else, nor to draw them into this conflict. For she knew her trail would be found sooner or later, and if it led close to the village then the nazram might suspect its people of hiding her. That would bring them into danger, and she would not have that on her conscience.

She came to the edge of the wood, and there stopped for a while. She looked back whence she had come, and listened hard. There was no sign of pursuit. So, she crept forward to the last few trees.

A faint breeze brushed her skin, and it helped dry her clothes which felt irritating against her body. So too her boots felt clammy and chafing. She stayed where she was a little while longer, and looked ahead into the more open lands beyond.

Like most of the fen, she could not see far. There was a maze of tall grasses, ponds, gulleys and higher tracts covered by trees. If the nazram were there, she could not see them. Nor could she see any tracks on the ground. Not recent ones, anyway. There were signs that several people had been here in the last few days, but that was likely the local villagers.

She sheathed her sword, and went forward. She dared not run any longer, for quick movement in the fens drew gazes toward it and she would more likely be seen. All the more so for this area was more open than many.

The sun felt warm on her, and her clothes were beginning to dry as she stepped out into the open and moved ahead. Checking the angle of the sun she changed direction slightly and headed due south. This would get her out of the fen as quickly as possible, and she knew the border of her home was not far away. Once out into the wider lands of the Cheng she would face different dangers, but it was death for her to remain in her home.

That was a thought that slowed her steps. How could it be that she was sentenced to death in secret by one of the leaders of her own homeland? There was no trial. If there were, she would be proved innocent unless criticizing those in a position of power was a crime. But it *was* when the shamans held authority.

Yet she would return one day. To do so, she would need much greater power than she had now. She would have to have fulfilled her destiny. If that happened, let the shaman beware. Perhaps she should be a better person, but she knew she held grudges, and in this case at least she had good reason. He had tried to have her killed, and she would not forget. Nor that the nazram had been willing to carry out his instructions. No, she would not forget these things and let them go. Ever.

The day was wearing on. She covered as much ground as quickly as she could, and she tried to hide her trail as well. That was not easy though, and she had little confidence she would be successful. Once she got out of the swamp and into the grasslands of the Soaring Eagles she would have a much better chance, should they follow her.

A little after noon she stopped for the first time. She had nothing to eat, for her food was spoiled in the water. Yet she picked a place where water lilies grew, and the stalks of these were edible. So were the tubers, but she did not want to spend the time trying to find and harvest them.

It was an unsatisfactory meal, but it would help keep her alive and fend off the pangs of hunger. She thought of going to a village for food, for she had money. But again she determined not to put their lives at risk. Also, if her pursuers spoke to them they would know where she had been and when.

She slipped off along the dark trail again, for this part of the swamp was thick with trees. They were not oaks however, but a kind of tree fern that grew tall. It was an eerie place, and she had been here only once before. She slowed down and took her time to make sure she did not stray from the path, for it was barely visible. Yet here, as everywhere else in the fen, there were signs left by the local inhabitants to give a guide as to where it was safe to walk and where it was not.

Yet even as she came out of this strange forest and saw the edge of the fenlands close by, she unexpectedly came face to face with a group of men who sprang up from behind some tall reeds.

Her heart thrashed in her chest. These were nazram, but they were not the ones from earlier. That gave her hope, but only a little. Her hand dropped down to her

98

sword hilt, but she did not draw her blade. That might provoke an attack, but if they moved against her she would. They were too close to flee from.

The nazram were as surprised as she was, but they were well trained and instead of hesitating they drew their swords all at once in a whirlwind of promised death.

Still, Shar did not draw her own. Blades were not the only weapons, and words must be tried first.

"Halt!" she commanded, and there was authority in her voice. She had spoken loudly, but not overly so. It was the certainty in her tone that stilled the men rather than the loudness. She spoke as though she expected obedience, and that was a trick her grandmother had taught her.

Certainly, the men stopped. But their swords remained drawn, and one wrong word could ignite battle.

"You have come to kill me, yes?" Shar asked them. "You would try to murder me at the behest of the shaman?"

Most of them looked down at the ground. She was on the right track here to call this for what it was and to remind them of it. It was one thing to hear instructions from your superior, but another when those instructions were called out openly for what they were.

Their leader looked her in the eyes though, and he was a hard man, and cruel, if she was any judge of character. Likely enough this would not be his first dark deed.

"It's not murder if it's sanctioned by a shaman," the man said. "It's merely a lawful execution."

"There's nothing lawful about it," Shar replied, "and you know it. This is merely the will of the shaman because I offended him. Is that the sort of person you look up to?"

The leader signaled his men forward, and they stepped slowly toward her. She detected reluctance there, but not enough to disobey orders.

She had no choice but to step back. There was a giant tree fern there, and it would offer her some protection against a group. Yet still she did not draw her sword. The thought of spilling blood, the blood of those who should be her compatriots, was not something to be done lightly.

"Have you no honor?" she asked. "Six against one to commit a murder. And for what crime save questioning the shamans? Have you not ever questioned them yourselves?"

That last point struck home. The men hesitated again, for who among them had not thought at times exactly the things she had said openly?

The leader hawked and spat. "Don't listen to her. Do what needs doing, and then we'll go home and forget about it. The clink of the coin we're promised will sound sweet to your ears. Now kill her!"

Shar drew her sword in a smooth motion and assumed a guard stance. She was relaxed and poised, which was not what they had been expecting. Her confidence made them question how easy this would be.

"You'll find I'm not easy to kill, you know. I'm better with a blade than any of you. And while you might overwhelm me with numbers, how many of you will die doing it?" She pointed with her sword. "Will it be you?" She pointed again, looking the warrior in the eyes as she spoke. "Or will it be you, or you?"

Again they seemed hesitant, but their leader yelled at them.

"Kill her and be done with it, fools!"

The men moved forward with raised swords, and Shar took one last chance to try to talk herself out of this. Reason had not worked, so she would try humiliation.

"Are you dogs then, to yap at command? Will you go back to the shaman and lick his feet?"

It was a desperate effort, and there were some who held back. She read growing reluctance in their eyes, but others pushed forward. Behind them, their leader kept screaming. "Kill her! Kill her! Kill her!"

The time of words was over and Shar determined to sell her life dearly. As her grandmother had taught her, she went for the closest man first and with a lunge swift as thought her blade drove up into his stomach, twisted and then withdrew. His guts spilled out of the wound, and he staggered back, tripping over his own intestines.

From some deep well in her memory she heard Shulu Gan's voice. *Kill the first of multiple attackers in the most violent and horrible way possible. That will sow the fear of death into the rest, and doubt will grow in their minds. This will make it easier to defeat them.*

Her grandmother had claimed to have learned that from the emperor himself, and she believed it. He was said to have been a kind man, but the legends spoke of ruthlessness as well.

"Who's next?" she asked.

The eyes of the men were wide, but they were nazram and had known fights to the death before. They charged her, but she kept her back to the tree and engaged the closest again. He partially blocked the others from attacking, but two of them tried to come at her from the side. This would be a short fight. She could not survive long against such odds, but she vowed to fight on no matter what wounds she received. She would take some of them with her.

Blades flashed. Steel rang against steel. She defended against her main attacker, and kicked out with her leg at the knee of the one at her left. There was a crack, and he reeled away. But the one at her right nearly killed her with a lunge. Somehow she managed to deflect that blow and still dodge a strike from the man in front of her.

101

"This is what the shamans do!" she yelled. "They set clan against clan and warrior against warrior. They divide us, and out of the chaos that ensues they rule!"

Again, the attackers paused. But it made no difference. These men were under the sway of their leader, and all of them under the sway of the shaman. They had doubts, but they would not disobey. They moved in again, more wary of her but still ready to kill.

13. A Strange Land

Once more the nazram attacked, and only Shar's great skill kept her alive. And the tree fern, for without that they would have surrounded her. Already she had been cut on her forearm by the sharp edge of a blade, and her thigh had been nicked by a sword tip.

This was a desperate fight for life, but at the end of it there could only be death. From behind the nazram their leader shouted at them to kill her, and he even laughed as one stroke of a blade nearly decapitated her.

That laughter suddenly turned to a scream. The nazram stepped back and swung halfway around, wary of her but unable to resist finding out what had happened behind them.

Shar looked also, and she saw the leader fall to his knees, his hands raised behind his head. He convulsed several times, and then he toppled down dead and twisted to the side. A dagger protruded from the back of his neck.

All the combatants were in shock, for this had come unexpectedly like lightning from a clear sky. Yet Shar, her reflexes and fighting instincts honed to a greater degree than her enemy's, did not waste time looking for the source of that dagger. Instead, she attacked.

The closest man to her was still half watching her, but her speed was dazzling and her blade severed the artery in his neck before he could even move to defend.

By luck, chance or fate, the situation had drastically changed. Now Shar leaped forward to bring the fight to them, but the nazram wanted nothing to do with it. They retreated to the side, and she saw why. Two men had joined the fray. One was a little man who looked like a peasant, and she instantly liked him. He was the sort of man she knew well, for he could have been a Fen Wolf. But he was not, and the style of his clothes showed it. He bent down to pull his dagger from the back of the dead leader's neck. He had no doubt thrown it, and thereby saved her life.

The other man stood close to him, and he was the opposite. He was dressed in fine clothes and his sword was of a type that she had never seen, but her grandmother had described its like. It was worth more than all the money in Tsarin Fen combined, and then multiplied several times. He was of the nobility, yet he used his blade with sublime ease. A man fell before him, dead before he even hit the ground and the strike had been so fast that Shar had barely seen it.

She knew who he was, if not the other. This man could only be the legendary Asana. He was the finest swordsman in all the land, and she had heard many stories about him and his description.

The remaining nazram grouped together, but fell back.

"Do none of you men believe in a fair fight?" Asana asked. "Or are you all just murderers?"

No one answered, but the little man drew close to Asana, and he lifted up the dagger. Blood still stained the blade, for he had not cleaned it.

"I say we kill them all," and he flipped the knife in the air and caught it deftly with his other hand.

"Perhaps that would be for the best," Asana replied. "Then again, maybe only killing one more would sufficiently make our point. It's a conundrum."

A man at the back of the group took a horn that was held by a strap around his shoulder and blew a long note on it.

"He calls for help," Shar said, and she went to stand beside her two helpers.

"No doubt," Asana replied, and then he faced the nazram. "But I give you fair warning. We will be on our way, and when your friends come, do not follow us. Or you will perish." He swept his blade around to indicate them all. "Every one of you."

"This isn't over," one of the nazram replied.

"Then come and fight me, man to man," Asana said.

The man did not reply to that, but he gestured to his fellows and they moved back into the tree ferns and disappeared.

Asana turned to Shar, and for all that he had just been in a deadly fight he seemed as tranquil as a kitten sleeping in the winter sun. His clothes were immaculate, and he breathed no deeper than a man sitting in a chair before a hearth. She marveled at him, but was even more surprised when he addressed her.

"Your name is Shar?"

"How could you possibly know that?"

He grinned at her, and offered a bow deeper than politeness indicated.

"It's a long story. Too long to tell now, so I suggest we leave here instead. Will you allow us to accompany you?"

Shar thought quickly. She did not know who these men were. Not really. Even if one of them was the legendary Asana, what did she really know about him except fireside tales? Yet they had saved her life, and it was still at risk. Only a fool rejected help when it was graciously offered.

"Of course. If you wish to, but the nazram will not give up so easily, and there are more of them. To journey with me is to court death."

Asana shrugged. "If I die, I die. I think those nazram will be wary now, though."

105

They cleaned their weapons of blood, using the tunics of the dead men.

"A good fight, hey?" the little man asked her.

"One that I would have lost without your help," Shar answered. "So thank you."

"Think nothing of it. Truth be told, I was ready for a little excitement. The last few weeks of travel have been duller than a rusted sword."

"Which direction shall we go?" Asana asked her.

"I was heading south," Shar replied, sheathing her blade.

"As good a direction as any," he answered.

They set off, walking swiftly and keeping a close eye on their backtrail. There was no sign of the nazram, but Shar did not believe she had seen the last of them.

"Are you Asana?" she asked.

"I am. And my friend is Kubodin."

"I want to thank both of you. You really did save my life, and I owe you."

They merely kept walking, Kubodin whistling out of tune and Asana offering a shrug and a short reply.

"You owe us nothing," he said. "You were doing well against them from what I saw. Very well. You have rare skill with a sword, and you might even have beaten them all by yourself."

Shar felt a flush of pride. The legendary Asana had said she had skill. He would not say that unless he meant it. But she put the feeling of pride aside. What skill she had was due to her training with the leng-fah, and then to her grandmother who took it to a higher level. Whatever skill she possessed was thanks to them.

She did not think he was right about the rest. "They would have killed me," she said. "I could not have beaten them all. At least I don't think so."

Kubodin stopped whistling and peered at her thoughtfully.

"Asana is a good judge of such things. He might be wrong though. He often *is* wrong about many things, but not that. You have great skill, but you were calm too. Few are the warriors who can achieve that, but that is what is needed to survive such situations. The mind is a stronger weapon than the blade."

The little man began to whistle again as they kept going, and Asana merely smiled softly at the jibe directed at him. These two seemed a strange pair, but Shar thought they were the closest of friends.

She considered what Kubodin had said. He had the look about him of one who had survived many battles, and he knew what he was talking about. His words unsettled her though. She *had* been calm. She always was in moments of danger, and she knew that was not normal. *She* was not normal. It seemed to her that danger made her blood run cold, and her mind cleared. The worse it was, the clearer her mind became and she could make calculations based on reasoned judgement and not fear or emotion. That was *not* normal at all, and she wondered why she was different.

Worse, she had recently killed men. Should that not worry her? It did not. They had tried to kill her, and she had fought back and survived. That was all. But that was a cold and logical way of looking at it. It was a warrior's way of looking at it. More than anything, it was the right way of looking at it. Yet had she lost something through all her training? Had she lost some part of her humanity? Had she lost something of what it was to be female, and to create rather than destroy? Her training had made her into iron, but iron did not feel.

Or maybe she was born that way, and it was an inheritance of a trait that had made her great forefather what he was. These were all questions she had no answers for, and it served no purpose to expend energy contemplating them now. Yet she felt the irony of that, too. For it seemed to her that something was amiss with that reasoning.

Yet she was who she was, and she cast these questions away. There would be another time to answer them. All that mattered now was escaping the fen, and that seemed imminent.

They came to a clear patch of ground. It was not even wet, but merely a stretch of solid earth well covered by turf. She had not been to this exact location before, and was not sure what to expect. But they came quickly to another patch of trees. These were oaks as was common in the fen, but they were not stunted and twisted. They grew tall and stately, and having passed through them there was only open grassland beyond.

Asana paused and studied the flat terrain ahead. Shar did so too. Then she cast her gaze beyond the wide, green expanse. On the far horizon were mountains. The range was known as the Eagle Claw Mountains, and within them rose up Three Moon Mountain.

She had no wish to go that way. First was the Soaring Eagle Clan. Then the fabled home of the shamans. No, she did not wish to go that way at all, but she could not go back.

"I see no sign of anyone," Asana said.

"Me neither," Kubodin confirmed.

So it was that they moved out onto the grassland, and Shar felt a strange sensation. She was leaving her home behind, and she did not know if she would ever return. She looked back. Everything was familiar to her, and she knew every smell and every sound. She committed them to memory, but the same could not be said for what lay ahead. She knew little of that, yet was it not part of the Cheng Empire of old?

They moved ahead quickly, and Shar felt exposed. There was no cover. There were no trees. There was nowhere to hide, and she had enemies out here as well as behind. But even as all the various lands were one under the name of the Cheng, were not all the different clans, just as she was, all Cheng?

That was how it should be. The shamans had used the centuries to cultivate the differences between the clans though, and to sow dislike and distrust. In theory, she should be safe here as a hunter for the twin swords. Free passage was given to all on the quest, yet bandits did not respect the protocols. And there were entire tribes that could be considered as bandits.

She left the fens with a sense of loss. Where was the call of the moorhen? Where was the howl of the fen wolf? She even missed the smell of wetlands. Yet at the same time something new beckoned, and there was so much in the world that needed fixing. By whatever quirk of fate that decided such things, destiny had given her a chance to shape the world anew. If she were strong enough.

They passed the night in the open, and Shar marveled at the stars above. She was not used to seeing the whole expanse of the sky revealed and the numberless stars scattered like sparks from a fire across the great dark. She wanted to talk to Asana and Kubodin, for she had questions for them. Yet she was deeply tired and slept after a hurried meal, eaten cold for they risked no fire.

Dawn came in a rush over the empty grasslands, and with it bad news. Kubodin spotted it first.

"Your friends did not take Asana's advice," he said, pointing northward toward the fen.

Shar saw what he meant. In the distance, and a long way away, she could vaguely see a group of men emerge from the dark green of the swamp. Here and there was the glint of metal, no doubt from the tips of spears. Few warriors among the Fen Wolves wore body armor or helmets. But it seemed to her that they had grown in number since yesterday. Perhaps there had been a third force sent to look for her.

"Time to be going," Asana said casually. "We still have a good lead, but we want to keep it that way."

Shar agreed. It seemed her words had really cut the shaman deep, and he would risk anything, or at least the lives of the nazram, to see her dead. That was for her to deal with though.

"I want to thank you," she said. "I want to thank both of you. But this isn't your fight, and there's no reason to risk your own lives. You have no obligation to travel with me, and you're obviously free to go elsewhere. I think you *should* go elsewhere."

Asana looked at her keenly, and she sensed a great intellect behind that gaze weighing her up. Then he merely offered her one of those little shrugs that he was good at.

"We choose to come with you, if you'll have us."

Kubodin only laughed. "I think traveling with you will be fun. I see lots of fights in the future! And travel without excitement is boring."

They moved out then, and Shar thought about her companions. They had known her name, but how? They were willing to share her danger, but why? This was not the time to ask those questions though. Soon though, very soon, she would get to the bottom of those issues. She had a quest to achieve, and she could never ask them to help with that. And if they wanted to, why should she trust them? They had saved her life, but that could be for their own purposes.

The sun was rising on their left, and a cool breeze blew down from the mountains far ahead. She checked behind

110

them regularly, and it seemed to her that the nazram were gaining ground. They must be breaking into a trot at times. If so, they would tire themselves out before any fight. Yet if they did not, then they would never catch up to those they pursued. It was a slight advantage to Shar, but it did not compensate for their greater numbers. They did not need to be fresh if they outnumbered their opponents by as much as they did.

It was not long before another problem arose. It was Asana who spotted it this time.

"There are Soaring Eagle tribesmen ahead," he warned.

Shar did not see them at first because they were still. There was no reason for them not to be, for she and her companions were heading straight for them.

"Shall we veer to the side?" she asked.

"Do you think we can lose both them and the nazram?" Asana replied.

She knew the answer to that, and she did not like it at all.

"No."

"Then I suggest we keep going straight toward them. Show no fear, and be friendly when we meet them. At least, that's my advice. After that, what will be will be."

Shar thought on that. She was on quest, and she had wrapped some white cloth around her arm last night, such an armband being the accepted means of signifying that she searched out the swords of the emperor. She should be safe. Maybe. And to try to evade them was certain to make them follow. What she did not understand was why someone like Asana was seemingly willing to defer to her. He had only offered the idea as a suggestion.

"I think you're right," she agreed.

They moved over the grassland quickly, and the Soaring Eagle warriors came into clearer view. As it was

111

evident that those they watched were coming to them, the warriors even sat down and rested. It was not a good sign, for that might be taking the opportunity to rest before battle. Yet Shar knew she was overthinking that. Why should they not rest, regardless of their intention when the two groups met?

It was not long before they came into close proximity. The warriors stood again, and there were some twenty of them. Too many to fight, yet Asana was reputed to have faced worse odds just by himself and lived. But that was just a story told over campfires.

"Remember," Asana muttered quietly as they drew near, "show no fear."

The leader of the group stepped forward, and his hand touched his sword hilt. He was a tall man, or at least taller than what was usual in the fens where starvation often stunted growth.

"Who travels the grasslands of the Soaring Eagle Clan?"

Asana offered a bow to him, and he kept his hand well clear of his sword.

"This is Shar," he said. "She quests for the twin swords of the emperor. And this is Kubodin, from the Wahlum Hills."

The other warrior studied them all, and Shar held his gaze with confidence. Then the man turned back to Asana.

"You keep strange company. Those hills are far away, even if the fens are not. Who are you? You gave no name to yourself."

"I am Asana."

The Soaring Eagle leader studied him. There was doubt on his face, and he voiced it.

"A name of high renown, but one that anybody could claim. Can you offer proof?"

Asana seemed tranquil as a summer breeze in a lush meadow, but swift as thought he drew his blade with a hiss from its sheath and crouched into a fighting stance. The move was so fast that even Shar had trouble following it. But he was once again still and tranquil, though his sword spoke of death.

The Soaring Eagle tribesmen drew their own blades, and warriors that they were they seemed like clumsy oafs by contrast to how smoothly Asana had moved.

Their leader remained where he was. He alone of his men had not drawn his sword, and he slowly raised his hand and gestured to them. They sheathed their blades.

"I am Tarok," he said, and offered a deep bow to Asana. "I believe you are who you say you are."

Asana did not move. His face showed neither relief nor aggression. He was like a sapling bent in the breeze, ready to move as circumstances dictated and then to spring back, unruffled by anything the world could throw at it.

"And do we have your friendship, Tarok?"

There was a pause, then Tarok answered. "Your name is honored among our clan, and you have our friendship. So too those who travel with you."

Asana sheathed his blade, and Shar noticed how he made even that gesture sing with grace and athleticism. What followed was a quick description by Asana of what was happening, and that they were pursued. He emphasized that a group of nazram were following them out of the fens to try to kill Shar.

Tarok asked her why this was so, and she sensed that much hung on her answer here. Yet there was nothing to do but tell the truth, and say that it was because of her criticism of the Fen Wolf shaman. It was an answer that might cause them much trouble, but if the Soaring Eagles were anything like her own clan then her words might find friendly ears. Whether that was so or not, it was better not

113

to try to dissemble. Tarok was one who looked at her with a clear gaze, and there was little that she could hide from him even if she wanted to.

When they were done, and Tarok and his men had looked into the distance and seen the approaching nazram themselves, they went apart a little and discussed matters among themselves.

It was a short conversation, and it seemed that Tarok had spoken for something, and the rest had agreed swiftly.

Tarok returned, and his face was grim yet Shar detected a glimmer of anticipation in his eyes. She resisted the urge to lower her hand to her sword hilt.

"The nazram have entered our lands unheralded," Tarok said, "which they should not have done. Yet though they have entered, they will not leave." He bowed gracefully to Asana, and then addressed Shar. "Good luck on your quest. It's time the Twin Swords were found. The world cries out for the one who can wield them."

With those unexpected words, he and his men moved off in the direction of the nazram, and Shar knew that she was not alone in her desire to see the rule of the shamans destroyed.

14. The Summoning

Shulu Gan knew the fen better than anyone living. She had known it of old, and she had renewed that acquaintance from time to time over the generations of the emperor's descendants that she had guarded. So it was that she had eluded the nazram searching for her. Whether they intended to kill her, or just question her at the behest of the shaman, she did not know. Or care.

They had forced her into a dangerous part of the swamp though. There were beasts here that could kill an unwary man, and even people in the nearby villages refused to come here, though game and fish were plentiful. Worse than the beasts were the rumors of magic, and she knew, better than all others, the truth of that.

There were powers in the world that shaped it, and there were creatures of the old world, of the world during the Shadowed Wars, that yet lived. They shunned humanity, for humanity was numberless and they were few. Yet here, in the heart of the swamp, where it was dark and secret, a few men stood no chance against the hatred that had endured for a thousand years.

She was by herself, yet she had no fear. These creatures were wiser than the shaman, and they knew her power. They shunned her, and slunk away from her as she traversed this dark stretch of territory. She was safe from them, at least for the moment. But of late she had felt her power fading and age, long held at bay, creeping up on her.

It was not important. As long as she lived to fulfill the mission she had given herself long ago, nothing else mattered.

She stopped beneath the shadows of an oak, shriveled and blackened by fungus. It was dead, but the skeleton of its branches reached out over a small pond, covered in green scum that made the water seem like mossy ground. There would be real skeletons beneath the water, for though few came to this place there were some from century to century, and some of those would have mistaken it for land. It was one of the traps set in this place to snare humanity by those who dwelt here that were not human.

Sitting down, she leaned her back against the tree and rested. She was little more than a skeleton herself, and the strength of her body was less than it was. Yet her mind was sharp as it ever had been. Even so, she could not read the future properly, or even some of what was happening now. Who was the Ahat after? Had the shamans discovered her after all these years? Or had they learned who Shar was? Most of all, was Shar truly destined to fulfil the prophecy of the dying emperor?

Shulu wished it was so, for of all the descendants it was Shar who reminded her most of her great friend of long ago. But maybe the years had clouded her judgement there.

Her thoughts went in circles, for she had no answers. Yet there was a way to get them, perhaps. Although that way often instigated more questions than it gave answers. But what was the point of magic if it was not used?

She rose to her feet, and felt pain in her left knee. The rheumatism in that joint was getting worse, but she could still walk mile after mile on it. A spell of dizziness swept over her too, but that would pass. She must allow it to pass, and just accept it. To fight it, likewise to fight her pain, only made things worse. With acceptance came relief, and the mind focused on other things.

She breathed deep of the air for some time, stilling her mind from chasing after thoughts. They were still there; she just did not dwell on them. In the same manner she saw and heard the world around her, but she paid it no heed. Stillness in the Storm warriors called it, those few of them who could achieve it. The Heart of the Hurricane the shamans named it. It was that state of tranquility where desire subsided, acceptance rose, and the fate of a person, or the universe, or a grain of sand were of equal importance. Which was no importance. The river of time ran on and it would make all things equally insignificant in the end.

When she was tranquil and at one with the universe, she let her mind drift to the prayers she had learned long ago. Some called them spells, but in her state of tranquility it made no difference what they were called. Her mind caressed them, and her lips uttered them, and her invocation floated away into the universe.

It would be answered. Or it would not be. The gods were not at the beck and call of humanity.

Yet a ripple went through her calm. She felt a presence gather near her and strengthen. The water in the pond began to seethe, and the scum that layered its surface began to shudder and separate.

Out of the dark water a figure rose, but she could barely see it. Mist came with it, and it swirled through the swamp and blanketed all. It was cold and clammy, and magic lived within it like the stars filled the midnight sky.

Why have you summoned me, Shulu Gan?

It was the voice of a god, and though Shulu had conversed much with the powers that formed and substanced the universe, yet still the voice cut through her and filled her with awe.

117

"I seek information about the future, O Harakness." For it was the god of water who had answered her call.

The mists swirled slowly, and the figure standing on the water of the pond grew at times clearer and at other times faded from view.

If you wish to know the future, you need only live long enough to see it, the goddess replied.

"No doubt, goddess. Yet I seek not to observe events as they unfold. Rather, I seek to shape them by my own hand and bring about fulfilment of prophecy."

Mist swirled about the goddess, and the changing and shifting of her form caused Shulu to become dizzy again.

What will be will be, Harakness answered, *and destiny will unfold as it must. The more you seek to control it, the more it will elude you. The more you seek to elude it, the more it will stalk you unawares.*

Shulu knew these things to be true. Likewise, she knew the gods saw more of the future than mortals. But the gods rarely parted with that knowledge.

"It is as you say, and I have learned that over the long years. Yet still, does not the woodcutter plan ahead how to fell a tree? Yet for all his planning the tree may fall upon him or somewhere else undesired. Even so, his work goes more smoothly the better his foresight has been. So, O Harakness, will destiny be fulfilled? Will Shar find the Twin Swords and lead rebellion against the unjust shamans?"

The goddess faded away, and then her figure grew brighter and clearer than it had been before. Shulu saw the white breakers of the ocean in her hair, and the storm-tossed seas flash and churn in her eyes. The sound of a gurgling river came to her ears, and then the mist shrouded all again.

Destiny hangs in the balance, the goddess proclaimed. *It can be fulfilled by the one you know as Shar, or it can fail of its promise.*

Yet know this. If she dies, the prophecy dies. For although others of the line yet live across the land, the old blood has diminished in them. Only in Shar does it still course strongly.

Shulu considered that. There were of course those scattered across the land who were related to Shar, for always she had nurtured the first-born child, yet others had lived and married. She even knew who some of them were, for she had followed what families she could over the centuries. She had hoped that if the worst happened to Shar then she could find one of the others and train them. Yet that hope was now dashed. Even so, the goddess had revealed that Shar was indeed the one upon whom destiny fell. She was the one the emperor had seen in his death-vision. The time of rebellion was now, and the fall of the shamans, if it could be achieved, was now, and now only.

It was all she really needed to know. Yet she asked one more question. She guessed the answer, but she wanted to *know*. The truth would not scare her.

"And what of me, O Harkness?"

The figure of the goddess became clear again, and almost Shulu thought she saw pity in her eyes.

You know that death beckons. You have cheated it a long time, but it is a relentless hunter. It may catch you soon. Very soon.

It was as she had thought, but the shock of those words still surprised her, and perhaps she was not yet ready to die after all. Even so, she straightened herself and looked the goddess in the eye. If she lived long enough to see Shar avenge her forefather and come into the glory that might be hers, it was enough. If that did not happen, then death would be a sweet release from the bitter injustice of the world.

"Have the shamans found me?" she asked.

Someone has found you. But you have lived long and made many enemies. Some yet live from long ago, and through the long years have

119

honed their hatred of you. But does it matter? What will be will be, and hatred is like an axe in the woodcutter's hands. It can destroy a tree, or just as easily hew into the man's leg by accident. It only takes one stroke in a thousand to go awry.

Those were not good odds, and Shulu felt a shiver run down her spine. She had made countless enemies, and many of the greater shamans knew the secret of the magic that gave longevity. It would do no good to ask more though. The gods were sparing with their knowledge, if they gave any at all.

Before she could give answer or ask anything else, the dark water of the pond began to boil. All about the goddess the mist swirled and the sound of the heaving sea boomed through the air. Over the churning water the goddess glided until she towered above Shulu, black as a thundercloud that drowned the light of the sun.

Shulu held her ground. It availed nothing to show fear to the gods. They respected courage and cunning instead.

Know, Shulu Gan, oldest of the shamans, that the gods stand apart from the troubles of humanity and heed them less than a man scrutinizes the lives of ants that crawl upon the earth. We will not intercede for or against you. Yet many of us do not look unfavorably upon the one you call Shar. This is a battle of humanity against humanity though, and the gods will have no part in it. Or should not. Fare thee well, and when the Great Dark overruns you at the last, remember that nothing lasts forever. Not life. Nor even death.

Shulu caught a meaning in those words that she did not like. The gods did not interfere in the troubles of humanity. Or *should* not. Was there then one or more who helped the shamans?

The goddess glided back over the water, and a wind roared through the fen. The pond emptied itself of water, spinning up into the air, and then it crashed to the earth once more and all was silent save the dripping of water off leaves.

Shulu felt a chill run through her body, and her heart fluttered irregularly. Talking to the gods was a dangerous enterprise, and she had learned little from it. But not nothing.

She sat back against the wet trunk of the tree, and planned what must be done next.

15. A Token of Trust

Kubodin spotted the cave first, and it was a strange thing to see.

Shar had not noticed it, for it never occurred to her that such a thing could exist on the flat grasslands. There were none in the fens that she knew of, and had she been asked she would have said there could be none here either.

The cave had a small entrance, barely wide enough for a person to slip through, even crouching down. It backed onto a rise, but that rise could not be called a hill. The inside of the cave was on a downward slope too. It had to be, for the cave could not be very big at all if it wound up into the slope. But winding down, it seemed to go quite deep. They explored it, and found several small openings at the back end that might go even deeper, but it was not wise to try to test that. Nor was there any need.

Dusk was settling over the land, and they had been looking for a place to camp. The nazram must have been dealt with, and they had no real fear of pursuit. But that did not mean there were not bandits, nor could they expect all of the Soaring Eagle Tribe to be as sympathetic to them as Tarok was. It was best to remain undetected if they could manage that, and the cave would also allow them a fire.

They were not the first to use the cave, for there were signs of old fires here, and there was even a good supply of firewood stacked in one corner. The grasslands were mostly open, but Shar had noticed a lot of small clusters of trees. There was one nearby, and first thing in the morning they would collect some dry wood and restock the cave. It was the rule of the wild for travelers to leave such a place as this in the same condition in which it was found.

The fire was burning well by the time night engulfed the land. Here, in the grasslands, the heat of the day dispersed quickly through the open sky and the evenings grew rapidly chill. It was not like the fens at all and the mountains were not far away either. Shar knew that though the land seemed mostly flat it did indeed tilt continuously upward toward them.

None of this was anything like what Shar was used to, but she had traveled as one of many guards before with the chief on trips to other clans. Those visits were done swiftly though, and it was different traveling with what was almost a small army.

The cave filled quickly with smoke, but it was not overpowering. No doubt there were cracks and crevices through which some of it escaped. More welcome was the ruddy light and its warmth.

They sat around the perimeter of the fire, and Asana heated some thin strips of dry meat. He did this as he did everything else, using easy and economical movements combined with a quest for perfection. Whether it was sword play, maintaining his appearance or cooking did not matter. He seemed to strive to do everything as well as it could be done.

Kubodin had loosed his axe and pulled out a whetstone. He sharpened the blades of the wicked looking weapon by turns, and the sound of that honing was unsettling. Already the blades were sharp, and they had not been used so did not need it. Shar had the feeling that the little man did this almost as a ritual rather than of necessity.

She took his lead and sharpened her own sword. It had certainly received use, and much of it. But as the smell of cooking meat grew stronger she gave that up and prepared for dinner.

They ate sparingly, for Shar had no food and the others divided what was meant to last for two into three. It was another gesture of friendliness in a series of them, but Shar was still not sure why they had helped her at all.

When they were done eating, she asked them. "We have time enough now for answers. Why are you doing all this for me? And how did you know my name when we met in the fens?"

Asana folded his hands in his lap and looked thoughtful.

"You're not the first person I've come across in the wilds and helped. Especially when I've seen a single person attacked by a group."

Shar could well believe that of him. "I don't doubt it. But there's more. And it doesn't explain how you knew my name."

"That's true," Asana replied. "On both points." He warmed his hands against the fire and was silent for a moment. Then he continued. "Kubodin and I would have helped you anyway, but we did have another reason. We know your name, but we know more than that. We know who you are."

Shar felt her blood turn cold. She was not sure what Asana meant though. Surely, he could not know her ancestry.

Kubodin kept sharpening the blades of his axe, but his movements were slower now and his dark eyes, glittering in the light of the fire, fixed on her own.

"You are Shar," Asana continued, "descended through the long years from Chen Fei, the great emperor of the Cheng nation. His blood runs through you, and if you can, you will overthrow the shamans and reunite the empire as one."

Asana finished speaking, and the cave was silent save for the crackle of the fire. Shar felt a shock run through her. These men knew who she was. They knew what had been kept secret all her life, and what she and Shulu had only discussed in whispers all that time. And there was a reason for that. If others knew, she would be killed. But now, others *did* know.

A moment she remained still while the shock of the words crashed against her, and then she leaped up and drew her sword.

Kubodin ceased sharpening his axe, but did not move. Nor did Asana. He merely gazed upward at her from where he sat, perfectly relaxed and calm.

Asana's voice, when he spoke, was soft. "Would you fight me, Shar? You know who I am."

"If I must," she said fearlessly, and gazed back at him without wavering.

"Why?"

"Because the knowledge you have spoken aloud is something I'm proud of. It's also my death sentence."

Kubodin began to sharpen his axe again, and Asana merely looked at her for a moment as though he were seeing her for the first time.

"You *would* fight me. And who knows, maybe you would win, for destiny needs you more than it needs me. But it need not come to that. We are your friends, and we are at your service. Like you, we distrust the shamans and know them for what they are. Like you, we would see them cast down and the empire rebuilt for the good of our once great nation."

Shar wished she could believe that. "Words," she answered. "Nothing but words. How do I know this isn't a trap and that you serve the shamans?"

Asana nodded. "If I were you, I would seek a token of trust as well. We were warned it would be so, and we were given such a thing."

This was something that Shar had not expected. She did not lower her sword, but she nodded.

Asana, careful to move slowly, drew something out from under his cloak. His hands covered it at first, and she could not see it clearly. Then he lowered one hand and held the object up in the light of the fire.

Shar knew it. She had known it all her life. It was the little statue in the likeness of her grandmother that had always been in the hut.

"How did you come by that?"

"You recognize it then?" Asana asked.

"I do."

Asana put the object down on the ground. Even there, it looked perfectly like a miniature version of her grandmother, even down to the eyes that glimmered at her in the firelight.

"Then you know," the swordmaster continued, "that it was given to us by Shulu Gan herself. She told us who you were, and asked us to help. And we agreed."

Shar was not quite satisfied. She asked them everything about that meeting. She learned all that was spoken, and when it had occurred.

"You know it isn't possible," she said quietly when they told her when Shulu had appeared to them. "She was in the fen then. I know that for a fact."

Asana did not seem surprised. "Yet she is a shaman, and her power is great. What magic she used, I do not know. But magic it was, and it *did* happen."

Slowly, Shar lowered her sword. Then she sheathed it and sat back down.

"This is difficult for me," she said softly. "I believe you. And I wanted to believe you even before I saw the statue.

126

But I have spent my whole life in fear of discovery. It isn't easy to accept anyone but my grandmother knowing who I am."

"We understand that, Shar. But if all goes well for you, one day the world will know who you are. Either way, you will be in danger. The two of us are pledged to help you though, and we are not without talents."

Shar felt a strange sense of ease coming over her. It was the warmth of the fire seeping into her bones. But it was more than that too. It was a sense of friendship and camaraderie.

The path ahead of her was dangerous. Every success she had, if any, would only increase her peril. Yet she had friends to rely on, and they in turn could rely on her. Two strangers knew who she was, but it was her task to increase that. It was her destiny, if she could fulfil it, to build an *army* that believed in her, or to die trying.

She stood again. "You know that to help me is to risk death?"

They nodded. "We have done that before," Asana told her.

Of course they knew. They had known since before they met her. Yet she had to say it. Then, reaching out to them in turn, she took their hands in the warriors' handshake, wrist to wrist. It was a pledge of equal loyalty. She could not help but wonder who they had risked death for before, and why. It did not concern her though, and now was not the time to ask.

She sat back down and looked at them again through the swirling smoke and ruddy light.

"You should know, before we begin, that everything starts with the swords of the emperor. I have to find them, but I don't know where they are."

Kubodin laughed at that, but said nothing. Asana, however, seemed thoughtful.

"Perhaps I can help with that. I know someone gifted with the Sight, and maybe he will tell you something of what you need to know. If he chooses to though, there'll be a price."

16. The Seer

Asana would say little more about the seer, for he said that he knew little himself.

They continued to head south, although now Asana led them just a little westward as well. They headed toward the Eagle Claw Mountain range, and Shar was grateful for that. Three Moon Mountain, the home of the shamans, was on the same range, but it was a little farther to the east.

She could see Three Moon Mountain though. There were days even from the fen, when the sky was clear, that she had seen the dark smudge of it on the horizon. It had grown larger as she entered the grasslands however, and she did not like it. It was the seat of power of her enemies, and she did not want to go anywhere near it.

They forded several rivers, and there were a great many streams across the grasslands too. The water was runoff from the mountains, and no doubt snow melt contributed to it as well. Spring was well under way, and the lower snows on the mountains had gone. Only the higher reaches were yet white, but some of those would stay white all through summer.

This was a land that Shar had heard many tales of, but she had seen little of it herself. Before long though, she guessed she would be better traveled than all back home in the fen, except for the nazram. And probably the shaman.

They saw no living soul. The land seemed empty and barren to Shar, for she was used to the closed-in environment of the swamp where life abounded. But they saw many signs of people.

There were trails, just as there were in the fen. They chose not to follow those when they came across them. Here and there the smaller creeks and rivers had fords that were built up of hand-laid stones. There were tracks of boots in several such places in the damp sand nearby. Mostly though, they saw only herds of cattle in the distance.

"Where there are cattle there are men," Kubodin said under his breath the first time they had seen such a herd in the distance. Asana evidently agreed, for he led them well out of their way to circle very wide around it. He did the same thing the next time they saw a herd as well.

Shar did get the feeling though that whatever patrols the Soaring Eagles had they would be close to where trouble was. Which was the fen. Here, deeper into their own lands, they would not patrol so much, or at all. So it should be safer to travel here. At least she hoped so.

They found shelter in a small wood just after noon. There they shared another meal and rested.

"Do you think the Soaring Eagles defeated the nazram?" Shar asked.

Kubodin chuckled gleefully. "I bet they did. The nazram tend to get lazy living the high life serving shamans. Those Soaring Eagle boys looked tough though, and eager for a good fight." He paused then, and his mood lowered. "A pity I wasn't there. I have my own grudge against the nazram."

Asana sighed, and Shar guessed that he was not overly fond of his friend's liking for violence.

"I think Kubodin is right. The nazram are dead, or else they have retreated back into the fen. Either way, you're safe from them."

"What about the Ahat?" Shar asked. After she had seen the token of trust from Shulu that these men had been given, she had told them about her encounter with the assassin.

Kubodin looked suddenly sober, but Asana did not change his expression.

"They're a different matter," the swordmaster replied. "But in truth, you don't know if they know who you are. Perhaps the man you encountered was sent after Shulu Gan. Or perhaps it was a coincidence, and you just happened to force him into a fight by discovering him when he was hiding."

"Both could be true," Shar agreed. "But it's stretching coincidence too far to think he was there for some other reason."

"Time will tell," Asana said. "If they *are* seeking you, they'll not be put off or killed as easily as nazram. They'll present a great threat, but not one that can't be overcome. And you have defeated one already, so that should give you confidence."

It *had* given Shar confidence. She had been tested against a swordsman superior to the nazram, and she had prevailed. But only just.

They traveled quickly across the grasslands for several days despite going out of their way to avoid any signs of people. Several times they saw large villages in the distance, usually preceded by plumes of smoke, but not always. Once, they even saw a patrol in the distance, but it was moving away from them and would not cross and discover their tracks.

All the while the Eagle Claw Mountains drew closer, and the land tilted ever more upward. It grew cooler too, and it especially seemed so to Shar. Her two companions merely grinned at her comments about the temperature.

131

They were not from the hot and humid fen, and they had seen far worse in other lands.

At night though, they had extra blankets in the small backpacks they wore, and Asana lent one to Shar. It was another of his small kindnesses, and Shar found herself really liking these men. They had skill, and courage. They did not shy away from hard work, and they were representative of much of the Cheng nation. The manipulating shamans and chieftains who lived off the wealth of those they ruled were the exception.

It was hard to say when they left the grasslands behind and began to travel among the mountains. It was a smooth transition from one to the other, but if anything gave it away to Shar it was a change in the type of trees. Now, most of the woods that they passed near were of pines, and she loved the look and scent of them. They were so different from what she was used to, and the novelty of them appealed to her.

"Are we still in the territory of the Soaring Eagle Clan?" she asked.

"More or less," Asana answered. "They don't come here very often though. Anyone we meet is more likely to be a bandit. Keep in mind though, there are bandits who flee injustice in their own tribes, and there are bandits who choose the life only in order to steal from others rather than toil honestly for themselves."

They traveled several more days, climbing high into the mountains. It was a strange place to Shar. The cold surprised her. More than that, it was a sparse land of few trees, barren slopes and slides of scree. There was so much space and openness, and far above the eagles circled in some slow sky-dance.

She was used to the opposite in every respect. Trees and water everywhere. Heat. The swift darting flight of a hawk. Yet despite all this, she felt her heart waken to this land. She was a foreigner in it, yet could she not learn its ways and secrets? Could she not come to love it if she lived here, and to appreciate its beauties? For apart from the strangeness, there *was* great beauty. At times she turned to study their backtrail, and she gasped at the vast vista opened up to her vision. It seemed to her that she stood upon a bank of clouds and gazed at the world far below. It was all open to her, and it was spread out like a cloth on a table and she could see it all.

She learned something from this. All the different clans in all their different locations over the land loved where they were born. That was home to them, and their home seemed better than all other lands. But it was an illusion. All lands were good in their way. Just as all peoples were good in their way. The differences should be honored and respected, not used to create a sense of superiority or inferiority. More than that, it should not be used like a barrier to build a wall between clans to keep each other out. Or worse, to keep individual clans ignorant of others and to pen them in like goats in a yard. But that was what the shamans did, who had for a thousand years known what she was just realizing now.

They came to a high ridge one day when the noon sun blazed coldly at them from a clear sky and a swift wind drove into their faces.

Asana led the way, for he had been here before. "Take care on this trail," he warned. "There's danger here if you misstep and lose your balance."

The trail was rocky, and it soon narrowed. On the left, a wall of stone grew up to tower above them, and on the right a ravine dropped away, steep and deadly if a person fell into it.

They went on, and in the ravine far below they saw a strange sight. There was a herd of some kind of mountain animal that looked part way between a goat and a deer.

Yet unlike any animal Shar had ever seen, they seemed to care nothing for the steepness of the slope of the ravine. No person could dream of walking there, but the animals ran and clambered and even jumped from one rocky outcrop to another. It was death to them to make an error, yet they did all this with careful abandon.

"Look there," Kubodin whispered, although the animals were many hundreds of feet away.

Shar followed the direction he pointed at, and she saw another animal strange to her. There were wild cats in the fen, but what she saw now was several times their size and nearly white. It was a majestic predator, nearly as agile as the other animals and stalking them silently from higher up the slope. But they saw or scented it just as it drew within range.

The deer-like creatures scattered, and the large cat pursued one of them. It was a game of death where not only the prey might die but the predator. Shar held her breath, and she could not believe the daring of these creatures to scamper and jump over a surface that was nearly vertical.

It was a chase that could not last long. The cat gave up, and stood staring after the creature it had failed to catch, swishing its tail in frustration. Then it turned and disappeared along some hidden crevice.

The company of travelers moved on, but Shar's heart still raced. The ravine grew even closer as the trail narrowed further, but Asana led them confidently ahead and soon the path widened again.

They came to a kind of barren plateau, but much higher peaks were visible all around them. The wind picked up even more, and there was sleet with it now. Shar drew her cloak closer about her and pulled up the hood. She was grateful to Kubodin for lending it to her, but the cold still bit through it.

"We're getting close now," Asana told them.

They followed the swordmaster, all with their heads bent low to protect their faces from the icy wind, and plodded ahead.

It was not long before the trail dropped down again, and there was another ravine. This was more of a crevice, though as they came close Shar saw it was so deep that the bottom was not visible. It was just a ribbon of blackness. It was too wide to cross, as well. Except that a bridge spanned it.

The bridge scared Shar. She was not used to heights, and this was far, far different from climbing a tree. Worse, it was made of rope, which she could see was frayed and roughened in many places, and some thin planks of timber. Trees up this high were rare.

"One at a time," Asana said. "I'll go first."

The swordmaster stepped onto the bridge with confidence, but he moved very slowly and each hand dropped down to hold the rope rails.

The span of the bridge was not far, but it took Asana some time to get to the other side. He hopped off it briskly, turned and called back to them.

"It's safe," he said.

For the first time, Shar was inclined to believe he was lying.

Kubodin went over next, and he showed no concern at all. He whistled as he strolled over, disdaining to use the rope rails at all. At the halfway point, he stopped to pull his pants higher, for the axe he looped through his belt always worked to pull them lower. Then he looked down over the edge, shrugged, and casually strolled the rest of the way to solid land.

Shar sought Stillness in the Storm, that state of dispassion that freed a warrior to fight without fear. It nearly eluded her, then she had it, and began to move across carefully. She did not look down. If she did, she knew she would panic. She had never been exposed to heights before, at least in this manner, and her fear was strong.

She thought of how easily Kubodin had done it, and then she understood he had acted so to help her. He had put on a performance like a storyteller and tried to show her that it was not as bad as it seemed, and her heart went out to him. He said little, but he was a man of deep and caring thought.

When she came to the halfway point, she stopped as Kubodin had done, and forced herself to look over the edge. Fear rushed up in her mind, but she forced herself to do this thing. Fear must be confronted, otherwise it grew and festered. Facing it down was like letting the sun in on the dark shadows of her mind.

She looked up at Kubodin then, hitched her own trousers up a bit higher despite not needing to, and winked at him.

When she came to the other side and onto solid ground Asana began to laugh loudly. He was not normally like this, being even tempered at all times, but when Kubodin laughed as well Asana doubled over and his eyes streamed tears.

After that, Asana led them around a rise and when they turned the corner a strange sight presented itself to them. Here, in the middle of nowhere where there were few signs that people ever came at all, was a group of stone buildings. One was larger than the others, and it seemed very grand to Shar who had never seen a stone building before. Yet she still noted the signs of wear and tear, and on the walls the stone had been eroded by wind or rain. That would have taken a long, long time.

"This was once a type of monastery," Asana told them.

Shar could not take her gaze away from the sight. "It's as big as an entire village back home."

"There's only a single man living here now," Asana told her. "If he still lives at all. He was old last I saw him, and this is a hard place to live."

But the man Asana had sought evidently still lived, for the door to the largest building opened and a figure appeared there.

The travelers moved toward him, and he showed no fear in this lonely place.

"He must have seen us coming from one of the higher windows in the building," Shar said.

Asana shook his head. "He may have seen us, but not that way." He said no more though, and Shar was not sure what he meant.

However, as they drew close Shar understood. The man was blind, for his eyes were milky white and he held his head as though listening to their approach rather than watching it.

"Asana, my boy. Welcome back." The voice of the old man was frail and wheezy. He looked even older than Shulu, though Shar doubted he was anywhere near that age.

The swordmaster bowed deeply. "Greetings, old father. It's good to see you again."

"And it's good to hear your voice, my boy."

For all that the old man seemed frail and ancient, he spoke with a spark of joy in his voice and his air was one of complete contentment. Shar had heard of holy men before. They were men who lived apart as hermits and sought a simple life of tranquility. It seemed this was such a man, and there was some force that radiated from him like warmth from the sun. Yet she did not doubt that there was a hard edge to him to. To live here, by himself and blind, required it.

"This is my friend, Kubodin," Asana said.

"Ah yes," the old man replied. "I've seen you and your axe walk the world. Be wary of it, my son."

Kubodin bowed. "So I have been told before, old father. And I will."

Asana turned to Shar to introduce her, but the ancient hermit spoke first, and she felt an uncanny sensation as those milky eyes locked on her gaze as though he could see her after all.

"I am humbled that you come to my abode, emperor-that-could be."

Shar felt a shock run through her, for there was no way he could know her ancestry. Yet he did.

"I am humbled that you receive me in your home," she answered politely and without allowing any of her surprise and uncertainty to appear in her voice.

The old man laughed. Then he swept away from them and back through the door. "Follow me," he commanded. "I've prepared a small meal for us."

Again, it was like he could see, for he stepped confidently and without the use of a stick. He passed through the middle of the open door, and led them into his home.

It occurred to Shar that while this man might not be able to see with his eyes that maybe some force of magic was used to the same end. Her grandmother had often said that the uses of magic were limitless.

They passed through a long and narrow corridor, and Shar felt a chill. This was a monastery, or had been built as such, yet she had learned of fortifications and how to defend or besiege them all her life. She knew at once that this was a killing ground for any who broke through the door. Tapestries, old and worn, covered the walls, but behind them she had no doubt that there were many slits in the stone to allow archers to ply their skill on intruders.

Her thoughts were reaffirmed when they came to the end of the corridor. A great door stood here also, intended to halt or slow the progress of intruders while the arrows did their work. But the door was ajar now, and a wide room with a domed ceiling lay beyond.

In the center of the room, beneath the peak of the dome, an ancient table was set with food and cutlery. It did not escape Shar's notice that there were four plates.

"Eat. Refresh yourselves," the old hermit urged them.

This they did. The food was strange to Shar, and mostly vegetables. Somewhere nearby the old man must have a garden, for surely no traders came this way. But perhaps there was a small village somewhere near, and they brought food to him.

They ate a pleasant meal, though the old man seemed to eat very little himself. There was only water to drink, but it was fresh and tangy and Shar realized the juice of some fruit was blended lightly with it.

Conversation was limited while they ate, but when they were done it turned toward the purpose of their visit.

"Do you know why we have come, old father?"

The hermit's milky eyes fixed on Shar, and he answered.

"I know. You seek the twin swords of the emperor."

"Do you know where they are?" Shar asked.

"Of course."

"Will you tell me?"

The hermit kept looking at her with those sightless eyes, and it was disturbing.

"Why should I tell you what I have never told others. And there have been many over the years who asked. Or tried to force me."

"I would not try to force you," Shar replied. "Yet my need is great, and I ask you this in return. Why should you not tell me? You know who I am."

139

The hermit tilted his head in thought. "A better answer than most, yet not good enough. I am very old, and I seclude myself from the world. What do I care about your need, or the fate of shamans, clans and emperors? Nations have risen in glory and then fallen to dust while all the while these mountains are unchanged. Nothing changes here, and nothing is important here. There are only the mountains."

It was a strange answer, but Shar did not think Asana would have brought her here without purpose or a chance of obtaining the information she needed. Then she remembered he had told her something about this old man.

"If it is not enough that I am heir to Chen Fei," she replied, "what do you want in return for the gift of your knowledge? There must be something?"

17. For My People

The hermit sat back in his chair, and he sighed. "Long ago I gave up my place in the world. It moves on apace, but I'm still here in my island of serenity. I care nothing for the world, and it cares nothing for me. I suffer no anguish nor hurt, nor do I give succor to those who need it."

Shar did not think he was so holy now. He had found peace, but he had paid a price for he had lost joy to do so. Yet there were many among the Cheng who sought this state of detachment. The hermit was the first she had met that had actually seemed to have achieved it though.

"There must be something you wish, old father."

The hermit fixed her again with those milky eyes. "I have left all desires behind me now. Save one."

"What is it?"

"In my far-off youth," he continued, "I dabbled in the magics of the shamans and the sorceries that came before them, which were mostly lost even then. I struck a bargain with … it does not matter who I struck it with. But in my pride I gave up my mortal sight in order to see the future. I thought that I could achieve fame and wealth and admiration. And so I could have, but the burden of foresight wore me down. All I spoke to … I saw their deaths. I saw the betrayals that wounded them, and I saw the paths their covetousness would lead them down. I saw, and I despised them. I wished to lose my gift, but that gift once taken cannot be put aside. It is with me always."

Shar understood him better now. No wonder he had followed the path that he had. No wonder he sought solitude from the world and detachment. Perhaps she had judged him too hastily.

The old man massaged his milky eyes. "These eyes can never see again, yet the one thing I wish is to do just that, even if but for a few moments. For that, I will tell you what you wish. There is a magic I can invoke to take your sight and make it my own."

A cold feeling sunk deep in the pit of Shar's stomach, and she felt as though cornered by her fate.

"And if I agree, what will happen to me and my sight?"

The old man looked away. "The magic does not last long. Perhaps a few heartbeats. Perhaps a few minutes. No longer. Yet while it runs its course you will feel agony such as you have never felt before. And when it is done, your eyes may end up sightless like my own. Or not. The magic is unpredictable."

"I'll do it," she answered without hesitation.

Those milky eyes pinned her again, and she felt herself being scrutinized and measured.

"Think carefully," the hermit cautioned her. "The pain is excruciating, and you may lose your sight forever. Nor do you have magic, as do I, to ease that burden. Does it mean so much to you to know where the swords are?"

Shar drew herself up. "The swords mean nothing to me. Although I admit it would be nice to hold in my hands the very same blades my forefather held himself. But I would not endure pain or risk blindness for that. Not at all. Yet for my people, for the Cheng, I will risk everything. They deserve no less."

The hermit was silent for a while, then he reached out with his hands to take her own. His hands were old, and the skin on the back of them was rough and thin. She saw the veins in them turn and twist beneath the blotched surface, but his touch was strangely gentle.

"Close your eyes," he whispered. "And prepare yourself."

She closed her eyes and thought of her grandmother. What would Shulu have counseled her to do here? But there was no way to know.

The voice of the hermit drifted to her in the silence of the domed room.

"I advise you not to do this thing," he said, and there was sympathy in his voice. "Once begun, it cannot be stopped."

Shar shook her head. "Do it."

There was no answer, but the hermit began to chant in a language she had never heard before. He proclaimed some spell in a whispering voice, and the domed room took the sound and rolled it around, casting it to and fro until it sounded like many chanted instead of one.

Suddenly, his hands pressed down on hers. She felt warmth radiate from them, and then it crept up her arms. She knew what it was. Magic.

The spell reached up her arms and enveloped her head, and then it found her eyes and locked them tight. Had she wished to, she could not open them. Nor did she think she could draw away from the old man. His magic held her bound.

But she did not wish to. Pain could be endured, even if it was unendurable. And for the freedom of her people, blindness was a small price to pay.

It seemed to her that light flashed in her eyes brighter than the sun, but there was no pain yet. Slowly, that light receded, and she saw a vision. It was not her own, she knew, but the thoughts or memories of the hermit.

She saw a great fortress, and the shadows of night clung to it. Fear wove through them like fish swimming in water, yet there was light also. The building hulked against the night sky, dilapidated and ruined by the ravages of war and time, but the starry sky rained thin rays upon it, and the silvery moon, full but low in the sky, bathed it in faint milky light that reminded her of the old man's eyes.

The fortress brooded, and she felt menace within it as though something there hated her. What it was, she did not know. That it sought her death, she was certain of.

The vision swept away and she saw a land of hills and tribesmen fighting. She saw Kubodin, only he was not as he looked now but regal. His axe he held high, and blood dripped from it, and she saw what looked like the reflection of some strange being twisting on the blades. Again the vision shifted, and she saw her grandmother, but she was young and fierce. This was Shulu Gan as the legends spoke of her, and magic played on her fingertips.

Her sight darkened, but one last thing she saw. It was an old man, hooded and cloaked. He raised his head and she saw some of his face. He seemed kindly, and his demeanor was one of simplicity and ease. Yet she saw something else in the dark flicker of his gaze as he looked in her direction. He was not who he seemed at all, and there was something very wrong with him. What it was, she could not say, but she felt a deep hatred stir inside her. If she had the chance, she would kill this man. And that thought shocked her.

The vision shrank, and darkness took her. At the same moment she felt the hermit's hands leave her own and his voice, soft and calm, broke the silence.

"Look at me, Shar of the Fen Wolves, emperor-that-could-be."

Shar opened her eyes, and she could see. A thrill ran through her, and joy blossomed in her heart. The hermit was gazing at her, and his face seemed gray and older than it had been.

"The fortress that you saw has a name. Chatchek Fortress it is called. Know it. Fear it, for your death awaits you there, if you are not careful. But so does the first step of your destiny, for inside are the twin swords of the emperor. They have been hidden there for all the long years since his murder. The shamans fear to look upon them for fear of what they represent, nor will they move them. And there will they remain until one such as you has the courage to wield them."

Shar felt hope surge within her, but she asked no questions about the fortress.

"It was a test, was it not? There was never going to be any pain, nor would I lose my sight?"

The hermit looked away. "Of course, but I took no joy in it. Yet I had to be sure you were worthy and sought the swords in order to serve the land rather than your own benefit."

Shar understood. If she were in the same position, she would have acted similarly.

"Chatchek Fortress has a bad reputation," Asana said.

"Nevertheless, that's where I must go," Shar replied. It occurred to her that Asana knew this hermit, and perhaps one day in the past had faced the same test she just had. He had not told her, but she did not blame him for that. Had she known, the hermit would have sensed it, or perhaps even seen it with his strange gift. If she could not be tested, then he may have withheld the location of the swords.

"This also I may say," the hermit continued. "The fortress deserves the reputation it has. Death resides there, and has seeped into the earth and the very stones that men built up as a protection of life. It is a place of dark magic that draws on the blood of those who battled there, and died. So think not that the shamans trusted to that abandoned and forsaken place merely as somewhere to hide the swords. They are guarded too. The fortress is a trap. And the Quest of Swords is a trap too. Should an

145

offspring of the emperor have survived, the quest is meant to identify them so the magic of the shamans can kill them. Even I, who have the Sight, have seen you enter that fortress many times, Shar. But not yet have I seen you leave it."

18. Killed by Sword

Nefu sat down and rested. He had read the tracks in various places, including the desperate battle, and then where one person had carried a corpse and then hidden it in a bog.

He had retrieved that body to be sure, and it lay before him now, stiff, covered in mud but not decomposing very much. He supposed some people would be unnerved by this, but he was not. Death was his trade.

What did trouble him was that one of his fellow Ahat had been killed. Even the best warriors across the whole land were easy pray for an assassin. They, as had he, trained since childhood in the arts of killing. It would take someone very special to kill one of his tribe. Or someone very lucky.

He thought back to what the tracks had revealed of the fight. It had gone on some considerable time, and it had ebbed and flowed. There had been no stroke of luck there or a killing by surprise. His fellow Ahat had been hard pressed at the least. Maybe he had been unlucky in the end and fallen to some random ill chance, but that did not seem likely. All the signs indicated he had been defeated by superior skill that just wore him down, and given the size of the tracks and the lack of indentation, it had been a small warrior. No. It was not a small warrior, but a woman.

The whole situation had been puzzling. They had been given instructions to leave the young girl alone, and to kill the old woman. So there was certainly ill luck there. His comrade had been hiding, probably to avoid contact with the girl who he must have heard or seen coming, but somehow she had discovered him. Otherwise he would have let her pass.

However it all came about, the end result was the same. He studied dispassionately the dead body that lay before him. An Ahat had been killed in a fight. Who had the skill to do that? More to the point, what peasant living among this dead-end, mosquito and fly infested swamp, had the skill to do it?

It was a question for the Great Master. If the leadership of the Ahat even knew themselves. Maybe they did, and maybe they did not. They certainly only told those in the field what they needed to know and no more.

He kicked the body back into the swamp and waited while it slowly sank. He had to push it down a few times with his foot. This raised another question. Why had the killer hidden the body? They must surely know by the tattoos that the dead man was an Ahat. But what did it matter?

It mattered to him though. So far as he knew something like a score of Ahat had been given this mission. Clearly, he was not the first to reach the swamp. He may not win the prize in this, for only one Ahat was ever recognized as the killer of a target. He had one less competing with him now, which was good. Yet if these peasants discovered an Ahat was among them, it would frighten the target into hiding or protection. So it was better this body disappeared forever.

At last, all traces of the corpse were gone. But he still stood there trying to determine his next course of action.

His target was the legendary Shulu Gan. He did not fear her. He would kill her before she had a chance to evoke any magic. Yet he was still wary. Certainly it was not her who had killed the other assassin. There was no sign

148

of magic, and the battle had been one of steel against steel only.

But how should he proceed? Of Shulu and the threat she posed, he knew and understood. Yet this other killer was a danger to him. Especially so for he did not know who she was and she might catch him unawares.

He decided to move forward. He knew where the village was that Shulu Gan had been rumored to live in. It was not the first time over the years that she had been discovered, though she had never been found in time. Always there had been stories of an old woman, usually a witch in a remote place, who never seemed to die but merely disappeared. So the stories went, and then he stopped walking as another thought occurred to him.

Those stories often mentioned another. An apprentice, a grandson and sometimes a granddaughter. But often there was *someone*. Was that just random chance, or was it something more?

It seemed to him that it was something more. Those individuals, and sometimes the whole family, had often disappeared with the old woman. If they were some kind of specially trained protectors that she hired to guard her, who just disguised themselves as family members, that might begin to explain how a girl had beaten an Ahat.

Then a new thought flashed through his mind, and he felt a thrill of anticipation. What if they were not guards for her, but she was a guard to them? What if these people sometimes associated with her were descendants of the old emperor as legend claimed? The prophecy foretold as much, if the words of a dying man could be believed.

If that were the case, and he found this girl, killed her and tortured the old woman into revealing the truth, then his reward would be immeasurable. The Great Master of the Ahat tribe would shower him with gifts. The shamans would reward him with praise and gold. He would advance to the very top ranks of the Ahat and live like a lord.

Nefu smiled to himself and allowed those thoughts to buoy him. Yet the smile faded quickly. If he had pieced this together, why had the Great Master not done so? He surely had access to a lot more information and had a better chance of doing so. But no order had been given to kill anyone with the shaman. Quite the opposite. Shulu Gan was the only target, and unsanctioned assassinations were punished.

His heart beat slower. There was another possibility. Might not the Great Master have figured all this out? Could there be a reason he wanted Shulu Gan killed but not anyone with her? Might it not be that he sought the girl himself, and wanted to keep her alive and gift her to the shamans?

All things were possible, and Nefu felt uncertainty drape itself over him like nighttime in the insect-infested fens themselves, unwelcome and annoying.

There was nothing to do but go on. He would discover the truth if he could, and perhaps he would take the girl to the Great Master. That would earn him his reward, or death. The Great Master might not want anyone to bring him the girl. That would reduce his glory in the eyes of the shamans.

Dusk began to descend over the swamp, and Nefu had had enough of thinking and plotting. It was time for action, and the night suited him. He could travel through it unseen and unheard. Few in the Ahat were as good at stealth as he was. It was true that he was not so good with a sword as some, but stealth would serve him with Shulu Gan. She was an ancient woman, and he had no fear of her, magic or no. But by stealth he would find her in her hut and put a knife to her neck while she slept. She would have no chance to use magic that way. And under that knife she would tell him all that he wished to know.

All that worried him was that others might reach her first.

19. Their Enmity is Old

Shar and her companions had accepted the hospitality of the hermit, and spent the night in the old monastery. It was a strange place, being so large yet occupied by one man, yet that one man was stranger by far.

The hermit was at once holy, dangerous, fatherly, warrior-like, humble as a servant and proud as a king. She had never met anyone like him, and did not think she would again. She would miss him, but she had obtained what she wished, which was the location of the swords.

The next day they descended the mountain range, finding a path different from the one they had traveled up. Asana led them, and he was cautious like that. He did not think anyone was following them, but he took precautions anyway. Shar approved. The nazram were likely all dead, but the thought of an Ahat on her trail was disconcerting.

It was a fine day. The sky was blue, the air still and nature, if different from in the fens, was bursting to life around them under the influence of the spring weather.

"Tell me of this Chatchek Fortress?" Shar asked. "I think I've heard of it in stories, but I can't remember them."

They were seated around a small fire. Timber was scarce this high, but they had found the remains of a long dead shrub and its trunk burned well, giving off little smoke for anyone to see, and by its heat they cooked a small meal for lunch.

"I've heard a few tales," Kubodin said. "But where I'm from most of the tales concern our own tribe, or the neighboring ones. What do you know, Asana?"

The swordmaster, sitting cross-legged and merely staring into the fire, took a while to answer.

"I know much. More than most, I guess. One of the masters under which I studied came from that area of the land, and when training was done for the day and dinner eaten, he would sometimes tell me stories of his homeland." He looked away from the fire and toward Shar. "You'll not like them," he said.

"It doesn't matter," she replied. "What I like or don't like won't help or hinder me from getting the swords. So it's not important. But before you tell me any of these stories, where is it?"

Asana looked back into the fire. "The fortress isn't really that far from here. It lies to the north of where we are now, and a little to the west. To get there we'll have to go past the fens, on their west side, and then continue on until we come close to the ocean. I'd guess that maybe it's a three-hundred-mile trek."

It seemed a long way to Shar, but her grandmother had taught her much about the land, its peoples and how vast it was. It would take about a fortnight to get there, but given the size of the old empire, that might be considered a quick journey.

Some of the smoke from the fire, little as it was, got in Shar's eyes and made them itch. She resisted the urge to rub them, as that would only make it worse.

"All right then. Tell me about the fortress."

Asana fed a little more fuel to the fire. "There are many, many stories. It's an old fortress, and it predates the Shadowed Wars themselves. At least, so my old master said. This is one story though that will interest you most, and perhaps has the most bearing on your quest."

Shar leaned forward, interested in every word. There was something about Asana's tone that commanded her attention.

"A thousand years ago the emperor himself laid siege to it. He was not, of course, emperor then. It was early in his campaigns, and his army was relatively small. But about him was a core of fighters who had seen battle and been tested. They were fierce, and they were loyal to their leader. He had led them true, and they would follow him into the underworld and death, if he commanded it."

Shar felt a shiver up her spine at those words. The stories of her forefather always affected her that way, and she always marveled at how great the loyalty of ordinary soldiers was toward him. A pity that some of the chiefs had been different, and that the shamans hated him. History would have been so different if they were not jealous of his power and covetous of it for themselves. But what they could never seem to grasp was that the emperor only used that power to further the will of the people. The shamans wanted it to further their own ends.

"The legend," Asana said, "was that the fortress was old even then, and though the defenders were few in number, that the fortress had been built in a great age and it was near impregnable. So it proved to be, for the siege last a year. Even then, it showed no signs of being overrun."

"But obviously, it did fall?"

"Indeed," Asana replied.

"How so?"

"It is said that not only was your forefather a great warrior, and a general of sublime skill, but that he also understood diplomacy and how to motivate his own army, demoralize the enemy, and to use contrary opinions among his opposition to good purpose."

"What does that mean?" Shar asked.

"It means that he sought out some of the enemy who did not like their own leader and he bribed them."

Shar was not surprised. War, like clan politics, was a pursuit where all tools that came to hand were used. All that mattered was that the choice was effective. If not, another tactic was tried.

"It did not take long for the fortress to fall after that," Asana said quietly. "Those who helped him escaped what followed."

"And what followed?" Shar knew, for she knew what war required. She knew that help must be rewarded and hindrance punished. In that way the story would spread and it would influence other battles in other places. It was a message that would bolden those who would welcome Chen Fei, and sap the morale of those who intended to defy him.

"There was a great slaughter, and the fortress ran red with blood. No one escaped. Yet it is said their ghosts still linger in the place their blood was spilled."

Shar did not like it. She understood it, but did not like it. Nevertheless, she also knew she would do the same as her ancestor had done. If resistance were rewarded, then there would be more battles in the future, and they would last longer. More soldiers would die. In the end, being harsh was the greatest mercy.

That feeling of coldness came over her that she had always had. Usually, it smothered panic. But sometimes it smothered emotion. Was there something wrong with her to be this way? Should she try to change? Or was this her true self, and nothing to be changed any more than the color of her hair or the way she walked?

"What is done is done," she said. "And I fear no long-dead ghosts, no matter what grudges they have. I don't believe in such things."

Kubodin made one of the many signs against evil, and shook his head vigorously. But it was Asana who answered.

155

"Be not so quick to dismiss such things. I have seen that which cannot be, more than once. The world is a strange place, and a dangerous one. The spirits of the dead do not always rest, and these ones will have little love for you. Their enmity is old, and they will seek what revenge they can get."

20. The Truth of the World

It was warmer when the travelers came down onto the flat lands once more, and left the mountains behind them.

Shar felt as though she had grown. Her grandmother had taught her much, but at a certain point teaching must give way to actual experience. And she had learned more in the last few days meeting different people and journeying across strange lands than she had in the last year living in the swamp.

As always, Asana guided them. He veered a little to the west of the fen. To go back there was to die, and even to be found by a border patrol was a risk not worth taking. But as she knew better than anyone, the Fen Wolf patrols rarely ventured far out of their own territory.

Asana seemed to know where he was going, and she got the feeling that he had traveled most of the lands of the Cheng and was known everywhere, either in person or by reputation. Kubodin was harder to fathom. He said little, and she had certainly never heard of him. Yet it was clear that the two of them had traveled a long while together and were the best of friends. What his skill was at fighting, she was not sure. She had seen little, but she suspected he was as good with his axe as Asana was with his sword.

For two days they traveled, and they saw no one. There was smoke from a campfire to the east on the morning of the third, so they did not light their own and they swung around even more to the west.

"Are we still in Soaring Eagle territory?" Shar asked.

"No," Asana answered. "We've entered the Fields of Rah, and this is Nagrak country. Last I was here, there was little fighting between them and the Soaring Eagles, but that might easily have changed. Our best chance of moving through undetected is to follow the border. Few people live close to it on either side, and we really only have patrols to watch out for. But if the fighting is still at a low ebb, they'll be few and far between."

Shar tried to recall to mind what her grandmother had told her of this clan. Nagrak City lay to the west, and a long way to the west too. The tribe really only had one great city, but it was vast. At one time, it had served as the capital of the emperor.

The Nagrak were a short and stocky people, and they raised sturdy ponies. Those animals were said not to be fast, but they were also said to be able to trot all day and outrun any other horses over a distance. The people themselves were fierce fighters, and they favored mounted fighting over war on foot. It was also said they used a short type of recurve bow, and they had served as the emperor's cavalry. Fierce, wild but honorable Shulu had called them. Quick to anger but swift to help those they liked. Shar liked the sound of them, but it would be better if she could pass through this land unseen.

Only a few days into their journey, that wish failed. Shar saw the rider early in the morning. He sat several miles away to the west on his pony, and he did not move.

"What should we do?" Shar asked. "Will he follow us if we keep heading north?"

"A good question," Asana said. "What do you think, Kubodin?"

The little man lifted his hand to his head and shaded his eyes to better see the rider in the distance.

"I don't think he'll follow us. Instead, he'll give word to the nearest tribesmen and send a group of riders after us. We'll not get far before they catch up."

"Better to talk to him by himself then?"

"I think so," Kubodin answered.

Shar was not so sure that was a good idea. "Won't we just scare him? We outnumber him, and if we approach he might think we intend to attack."

Asana looked thoughtful. "That's possible, but I'm inclined to think otherwise. The Nagraks are a brave people, and he's on a pony. He can escape us easily, but more likely, if he thought we were a danger he'd kill us by bow shot."

That was not so reassuring to Shar, but she did agree with Kubodin. To try to outrun him, or those he called to investigate, was to court a greater risk.

They turned toward him and commenced walking in his direction. Straight away they saw the rider nudge his pony forward and the beast trotted in their direction.

Kubodin laughed. "I like him! He's not in the least scared."

"No," Asana replied. "He *will* have his bow though. Be wary of that, for though the weapons are short limbed they still kill, and these men are swift to shoot arrow after arrow."

The grass was short here, and they followed some sort of game trail, likely a kind of wild cattle as far as Shar could tell from the tracks. The rider was on the other end of it, and though his pony did not seem to hurry it closed the gap between them swiftly.

Soon the rider and the three travelers were close, perhaps only fifty feet between them. His bow was in his hand, but no arrow was nocked. Shar marveled at his skill, for he controlled the pony merely with his legs and left

159

both hands free to hold his bow and draw an arrow, if need be.

Nagrak gul sak viran, Shar called out to him.

The rider appeared to be startled, but he gave the reply to the ritual greeting. *Nagrak gul sak yohan.*

Asana raised an eyebrow at her, which was as much surprise as he ever showed. But her grandmother had taught her many things, and she knew the customs and dialectal phrases of all the many Cheng clans. This one was a greeting in the Nagrak Clan that signified a wishing of peace upon the other traveler, which was reciprocated.

The rider edged a little closer. "You know our ways, stranger?"

"I was taught by one who once knew them well."

The man studied her carefully. He was old but sprightly. The arm that held the bow was scarred by sword cuts, but the veins and sinews stood out. Once, he would have been a warrior, but in age he now likely herded sheep or cattle. She did not think he had forgotten how to fight though.

"Will you join me for nahaz?" This was what Shar was hoping for. It was a drink brewed out of mare's milk, and then distilled into a spirit. Sharing it was a sacred ritual among strangers that made them fast friends. It was a grave breach of honor to quarrel or fight afterward, at least for a day.

"We have none of our own to share, but we would gladly accept your hospitality."

The rider dismounted and went to remove something from his saddlebags. He did this carefully, still watching them with caution. They had not yet shared the drink.

Shar took off her cloak and rested it on the ground. Then she sat, cross-legged, gesturing Asana and Kubodin to do the same.

160

"Say nothing until we have shared the drink," she whispered to them. "It's considered rude to speak before the bond of friendship is sealed."

She was not sure if the others already knew this. She did not think so. Asana had been here before, but this was a ritual rarely shared among strangers from other clans.

The rider removed a flask from his saddlebags and unstopped it. He never took his eyes from them while he did so, and he kept his bow in a good defensive position. He was too close to them to use it as a projectile weapon, but that was not the only use of a bow. If something went wrong, it would be used at the least as a kind of shield until he withdrew the saber sheathed at his side.

The man sat, and carefully he handed the flask to Shar. She knew what nahaz was, but had never tasted it before. Shulu had told her it was disgusting, but she tipped the flask back and tasted it, masking any emotion on her face.

Disgusting was a mild description, yet she did feel it burn through her insides like fire and enliven her. She understood how this could have medicinal benefits, and she knew also that the Nagraks drank this spirit before battle.

She handed the flask to Kubodin, and the little man took a gulp. His eyes bulged, and then he chuckled to himself but said nothing.

Asana took a delicate sip, and what he thought of the drink was impossible to tell. He calmly handed the flask back to the Nagrak warrior.

The old man took it and eyed them all carefully, his gaze lingering on the white armband that Shar wore, and then he tipped his head back and swallowed deeply. When he was done, he eyed them all again.

"We are camp friends," he said, "but in truth you are strange even for strangers. Never have I seen such a group as you before, even during the Quest of Swords."

161

"We are camp friends," Shar echoed. "I am from the Fen Wolf Tribe, and this is Asana and Kubodin."

The old man glanced sharply at Asana, and she knew he had recognized the name but he said nothing.

"I am Nadral, but I see you do not give your own name."

Shar considered carefully. "I do not give it in order to protect you. I am hunted by nazram, and perhaps by Ahat. But my name is no secret from a camp friend if you ask it."

The old man looked at her long and hard. Then he smiled.

"Your name is Shar, and you seek the twin swords. The shamans have sent word across the land that you can be killed at will."

That was a shock to Shar, but she should have expected it.

"And will you try to fulfill their will?"

The old man turned away and spat. "I'd sooner drink nahaz through my nose. And there are many like me who are tired of the yoke the shamans place around our necks and call it kindness. But not all, so be wary."

They fell to talking then, and the old man gave them the news of the land as he knew it, which was limited because most such news came via the shamans and all was twisted to suit their purposes. Yet if the clans communicated little with one another, the shamans were well connected all over the land and news traveled fast, at least to them.

Nadral told her that she was accused of murdering a nazram officer. She in turn told him the truth, that many of them had sought to kill her. He studied her carefully again after that, then spat once more.

162

"I believe you. But you must be good with that sword otherwise you would be dead. Yet maybe you will be better with two?"

What exactly he meant by that, Shar was not sure. It was not possible that he could know who she was, and yet the prophecy was known to all tribes. Many longed for it to be fulfilled.

She asked him to spread the word of what she had said, that the shaman of the Fen Wolves had tried to have her killed and that he was the murderer, and that Asana, whose name was known throughout the land, vouched that her words were true for he had been there.

They parted in friendship after sharing a meal, and the warrior mounted his pony and trotted off.

"A good man," Kubodin said. "I like him."

So did Shar. But she could not be sure that others she met would be like him, and that worried her. Without doubt, others would recognize her by sight as her description had been passed around.

There was little she could do about any of it though, and they soon commenced their journey again. That worry was still on her mind several days later when they drew near to a small village. She did not want to go inside it, but at the same time they needed to buy supplies.

She made an effort to disguise herself, letting her hair down and borrowing a cloak from Asana that was much finer in quality than her own or anything that a Fen Wolf would be expected to wear. Likewise, the cloak mostly hid the sword she wore, which was perhaps the biggest indicator of who she was. Among the Nagrak, few women bore weapons other than knives.

They entered the village at noon, and it seemed to be bustling. It was a market day, and many goods and livestock were being sold in the main road, brought in from farmers and hunters for miles around.

As quickly as possible, they purchased what supplies they needed and then began to leave. The faster they came and went here the less chance anyone would recognize her or remember three strangers passing through.

At the crossroads in the center of the village though a crowd had gathered and they had trouble passing through it. A shaman was speaking there, and he seemed a fairly young man, but he was proclaiming with great fervor and his eyes were bulging with fanaticism.

"Listen!" he declared. "I hear rich men grumble at the taxes they pay, and poorer men grumble that they pay taxes at all. But know this! The shamans and the chief spend your money wisely, and all across Nagrak villages like this prosper! You know it is so, and you know your money is spent where it is needed. Even the poor must pay taxes, and the rich can afford many times more. In the end, we are all one and we all benefit equally. Trust that your leaders have your wellbeing in mind, and they know how to deliver benefits to you. Hide nothing when the tax collector comes to your house."

The shaman kept talking, but Shar ceased to listen to him. Instead, she looked at the crowd. There were some who cheered the shaman's words, and some looked back with the same fervor that he gazed at them with. For the most part though, the crowd looked bored. Some even looked angry, but they tried not to show it.

Shar looked at the people closely. They reminded her of the Fen Wolves, but just like at home poverty was evident. Women wore cloaks with holes in them, and many of the faces were dirty and their hair uncombed. The men were sullen and shuffled their feet, most of them wearing boots worn right down at the heel. There were beggars among them, no doubt once warriors, but some were missing arms and legs. Or eyes. The hardships of battle were many, but these were all malnourished as well, unable to work and unsupported by those who sent them to fight on their behalf.

A sense of anger rose in Shar, but she fought it down. If she spoke what she thought to the shaman she would only end up being killed. If she wished to help her people, not just the Fen Wolves but all the Cheng, she must find the twin swords.

She had never felt closer to her forefather than she had at that moment. She was proud of him, for she was beginning to understand the battle he had fought against the might of the shamans and the risks he had taken, all in the name of his people.

They moved through the crowd, but soon drew near to several others who wore the white armband signifying they were on quest. They saw hers also, and made to approach.

This was the last thing she wanted. They would ask questions and see if she had news. She did not want to lie to them, but neither could she tell them the truth. Also, it would make her stand out and be more memorable at a time when she would rather be as invisible as a shadow.

"Any news of the swords?" one of them asked as they came close.

"Not yet," Shar replied. "You're the only other questers I've met so far."

She tried to edge away, but they began walking with her.

"Where have you been?" the man asked.

"In the Eagle Claw Mountains," she said.

He frowned at that. "Why there?"

"One place is as good as another if you don't know where to look."

He nodded at that, but he seemed doubtful. She sensed that he was beginning to feel that she was holding back from him, which she was.

"Where are you going now?"

She paused a moment to think. "Westward, probably." She knew the moment she said it that it was a mistake. If they found out otherwise, they would know she was trying to conceal something from them. But her mistake was worse than that.

"We're heading westward too. How about we join forces for a while? We'll be safer in greater numbers."

Shar cursed her stupidity. She should not have given any direction at all, and now she would have to be rude.

"Thank you for the offer, but we feel safe enough. Anyway, my friends and I prefer to travel by ourselves. We can set our own pace that way and see where things take us."

The other man looked at her hard for a moment. He had no right to be offended, for surely most people on quest would prefer to be by themselves in case they actually did discover the swords. But maybe it was more than that and he truly began to believe she knew something.

"As you wish," he said with a shrug and moved away with his friends.

Soon they were out in the open space of the grasslands once more, and Shar began to get a sense of how vast the Fields of Rah were, for they had been traveling for some days and, once outside the village again, everything was the same as it had been. It was all just an endless sea of unchanging grass.

It felt too open for her, and she missed the fen. Yet this was preferable to the press of people in the village.

They had only traveled a mile or so when Kubodin grunted.

"Your fellow questers for the swords didn't take the hint."

Shar looked back, and her heart sank. The three questers were there, and all their witnesses. They had not believed her when she said she had discovered nothing of the swords, and they were following her. She cursed loudly.

"It's not your fault," Asana said, seemingly understanding the cause of her frustration. "Those who quest for the swords are known to do this. They always think their fellow questers know something they don't."

21. Watched

The three travelers walked swiftly, Asana leading them as always. They changed direction at times, and even tried a night march to lose those who followed them, but it was to no avail.

Shar did not like it. By following her, these other questers were endangering themselves, but it was beyond her control. At least they never sought to catch up with them.

"What happens when we reach the fortress?" she asked Kubodin one morning as they gazed back at their distant shadows.

"A good question. When they see it they'll realize that we were heading there all along. They might try to join us then."

Asana did not think so. "When they see the fortress, I think they'll fear to go forward. As will we."

They were dark words, and Shar got the feeling that the swordmaster had not revealed everything he knew, or surmised, about their destination.

Kubodin turned away from gazing at their followers and marched forward once again. "Whatever happens to them, it's on their head. Rabbits shouldn't follow wolves into the woods."

At last the flat and open grasslands began to change. They entered a country now of long, sloping downs. There were more trees, but all sign of people faded away. There were no tracks. There were no campfires on the horizon. There were not even any indications of game. It was a wild and rugged landscape, for the deep earth of the plains was gone and the tops of many of the downs were bare outcrops of chalky soil. This fascinated Shar, for there was nothing like it back in the fen.

Asana noticed her curiosity. "See how the trees have changed?" he asked. "They're beeches now, for they favor this type of soil and oaks do not."

The beech trees were new to her as well. They seemed queenly to her, full of grace and elegance. But they were quiet. She saw no birdlife as she would have expected in oaks, and the downs felt brooding to her as though waiting for a storm even though the sky was clear.

They made good time, yet ever their distant shadows kept pace with them.

"We're not far from the fortress now," Asana said. "Keep your eyes open. No one lives here, but there may be bandits who hide in such a place. Few would follow them into this land, and they are safer from justice here."

Asana did not seem worried about that prospect though, and they saw no signs of anybody else at all. The whole land was quiet, but it did not seem restful.

They continued on through the day, and the land was wild and isolated. Their followers kept pace with them, staying a mile or so back at all times, resting when those they pursued rested, and marching again when those they pursued marched.

The sun fell lower in the west, and the temperature dropped quickly during the afternoon. Shar walked ahead, as alert as she could be, and anxious for what lay before her. What if the hermit was wrong? What if he was not a true seer, and the swords were not here at all?

She did not like thinking that way. Either the blades were here, or they were not. Either she could claim them, or she could not. If she died in the attempt, then she died. If they were not here, she would look elsewhere. It was that simple, but with all her heart she wished the seer was

169

right, and that soon the hilts of those legendary weapons would fit snugly into her hands.

The day drew on and after a while Asana stopped and pointed.

"There it is."

It was not much to see, for they were still some distance away. Yet the outline of a fortress was there, shrouded in shadows from craggy heights that rose above it.

They kept going, and slowly the fortress revealed itself. It was certainly old. The ramparts had toppled in places, and here and there a tower had collapsed as well. Mostly the walls were intact though, and the towers still strained toward the sky.

Shar marveled at it. Her people had built this a thousand years ago, or perhaps even much further back in time than that. Yet it still stood, if worse for wear. Yet now, what did the Cheng build? All she had ever seen were wooden huts, and sometimes not even that. Perhaps in Nagrak City there were stone buildings left. She remembered her grandmother saying that. Yet they were remnants of the past too. How far had her people fallen? What could they build now? She did not think any were left who knew the arts of old, and she wondered too if that could be blamed on the shamans. They kept people divided against each other. Why not keep them ignorant as well? The separated and the poorly educated were easier to control.

As they traveled through the silent wastes, a feeling of unease crept over Shar. She felt as though she was being watched. It might have been a sense of those who shadowed them, but she did not think so. It felt like the land itself was aware of them, or perhaps just the fortress.

The building grew bigger as they approached, and she marveled at it again. It was huge. It was beyond anything

170

she had ever seen, and the sheer size of it alone was staggering, let alone the intricacy of design.

The fortress would have taken hundreds of men years to build. Maybe even decades. That spoke of a great king who commanded a large workforce, or army. It indicated a time of prosperity too, otherwise no such workforce could be taken away from the duties of farming and supplying food for a large and hungry population. But it suggested fear too. Whoever had built it had thought it necessary to devote an enormous amount of money, planning and time to its construction. Many things had obviously changed, yet the fear of attack was not one of them.

"It's bigger than a fat woman after the harvest feast," Kubodin said with a certain amount of awe in his voice.

Shar did not much care for his description, but she felt the awe too.

Beyond the fortress rose a harsh landscape of steep slopes and ridges, but much of it was swathed in a shadow-haunted forest of pine. Shar preferred the beeches. There was something sinister about those woods, and some nameless fear gnawed at her instincts.

She stepped forward anyway, not letting anything deter her from what she must do. If she began to think too deeply, she would never go through with this. The seer had as much as told her that it was a trap.

Looking at the battlements, she saw several places where the stone, or perhaps mud bricks, had collapsed outward in a heap right down to ground level. The two towers that guarded the gate were intact though, but the gate itself seemed a gaping hole as far as she could tell from this distance.

"At least getting in won't be much of a problem," she said.

Kubodin did not look at the fortress but kept trudging ahead, shaking his head and offering no answer. But Asana did.

"Getting in isn't going to be the problem. It's getting out that will be difficult."

22. Who Disturbs Our Rest?

They came to the fortress gate, and stopped before it. Massive pillars of stone framed it, but these were rent where the great iron bars to each side had been pulled loose. The gate itself had been attached to these iron bars, and though age had worn them through ceaseless centuries, and rust pitted them, each bar was a mighty thing thicker than a large man's arm.

Shar stood on the threshold of that gate, and the sense of awe that she had felt upon approaching the fortress struck her as a blow. Her heart leaped like a wild beast in her chest, pounding and thrashing. Her tongue was stilled, and she dared not speak. Cold settled through her like a blanket of frost, penetrating deep into her bones.

Her great forefather had taken this fortress. It was a structure that defied time itself. It was massive. It seemed impregnable. An army could cast itself against it and be thrown back like so many ants trying to level a mountain. But the emperor had done it, and the proof was before her.

The gate was twisted and bent, and it was thrown open and hurled back against the left tower. Scorch marks blackened the stone there, and some of the bars were bent. Even though deceit from within must have opened the gate, yet still a mighty battle had been fought on this very spot.

Then a new awe filled her up as though she were a vessel into which water was poured. Her forefather had stood in this very place. For the first time in her life, her boots sunk into the same earth that his had done. She saw the towers as he had done, and the gate itself. It was a connection to him like no other that she had ever felt. What had he been thinking as he stood here, where she stood now? What had he felt at the fall of the fortress? Did he realize then that for all his mighty achievements he would still die and become dust? Would she ever bear children, and would one of them stand where she was now and wonder what her life had been like as she wondered about his?

The three travelers stood in silence, and dusk settled over the land. It fell down from the forested heights like a vast blanket of shadow being tossed over a bed. There was a soft beat of wings above, for bats funneled out of openings higher up in the towers to each side. The creatures streamed out, circled and wheeled against the kindling sky, and then left it open again for the brightening stars to shine down.

"Well, now what?" Kubodin asked. "Shall we camp here for the night and enter the fortress when the sun comes up?"

Shar turned back to look at those who had followed them from the village, but it was too dark now to see.

"They know where we go now, and must suspect we believe the swords are inside. I don't think they'll shadow us any longer. Instead, I think they'll try to catch up with us. If we wait until morning, we'll be going inside *with* them."

Asana seemed doubtful. "What you say is true, yet I don't relish the idea of going inside during the night."

"Nor I," Kubodin echoed.

Shar did not either. Yet she straightened and spoke in a calm voice.

"You need not come with me. Yet I at least must go inside. And now. I have waited much of my life for this moment. I cannot wait longer. And I'll not let someone else try to claim those swords."

Kubodin pulled his trousers up a bit higher and withdrew his terrible axe from the belt loop that held it.

"I'll go with you," the little man said.

Asana spoke too, his voice soft. "As will I. Let our pursuers follow, if they dare."

They made preparations to go inside then. They would need light, and so they found some pieces of fallen timber nearby. Around these they wrapped cloth, though they had no oil to dip that cloth in. Yet it would help ignite the timber.

Their torches flared sullenly to light amid the growing dark, and Shar led the way forward. This was her quest, and she could no longer defer to Asana or allow others to go into danger first. This was her quest, yet as best as she could she would protect those who helped her.

It struck her as strange that the shaman of Tsarin Fen had forbidden any from the tribe to act as her witness in this task. Yet she had found two witnesses outside her homeland, and she could have wished for none better. Maybe it was good luck. Or maybe it was fate.

She stepped through the threshold of the gate as once her ancestor had done. The light of the torches flared brighter, then dimmed. Here, in the tunnel through the fortress wall that would have served as a killing ground in the battle of old, her unease grew. Soldiers had once entered here, and no doubt died.

It was not long though before the tunnel drew to a close. At its end, and near now, was another gate. This too hung in ruin from the stone wall that held it, even if only partially now.

Here she paused, knowing she must go on yet stilled by some sense of dread.

Suddenly, there was a screech of metal like the shriek of a soldier impaled by a spear, and it was followed by a thunderous boom. It sounded like the outer gate had slammed shut by itself, and the skin on the back of her neck crawled.

Silence fell over them again, but it was broken by a laugh from Kubodin, even if it was a grim one. "I guess we needn't worry about being followed in here. I don't think our friends from the village are invited to the party."

Shar knew he was using humor to try to ease their tension. It was an old warrior's trick, and at that moment she loved him for it.

All about them something moved now. The air was still, but *something* moved. It took form then along the walls of the killing passage. A row of warriors appeared, thin as moonlight, but the dark glance of their eyes was sharp as a blade. They gazed with hatred, yet though they wore swords they did not draw them.

It was the same on the other wall, and Shar wished she had listened to Asana and Kubodin. It would have been better to enter the fortress in daylight. It did not matter though, in the end. Come what may, she would retrieve the swords.

Shar stepped forward. A hundred ghostly gazes watched her, and that was all the more reason to show no fear. Even if it was her forefather's army that had killed these men.

She studied the gauntlet of dead men through which she walked. What tribe they were, she did not know. Shulu had taught her how to recognize most clans at a glance. There was usually some characteristic of dress or ornament that set them apart, but she could see nothing here. Yet still they were fierce warriors, and proud. It did not matter what their tribe was. If they had none, they were still Cheng.

176

She led her companions through the second gate and into a courtyard. Here too were ghosts, and there seemed thousands of them. They made no move. They said no words. Only their judging eyes shifted, following the path she set through the otherworldly host.

By the flickering light of the torches she could see ahead. There was an inner keep to the fortress, and it seemed that the ghosts had left a path open in that direction. It was where she would have gone anyway, but that *they* seemed to want her to go there was disturbing. Was this the trap the seer had warned of?

The ground they trod was unsettling. It was not level, though she thought that some kind of brick paved it. Yet the surface was covered in dirt and a few straggling weeds. And more, for she saw at times a rusted sword or piece of armor, and even bones. Worse than bones though were the skulls, leering up at her from their empty eye sockets, and their dark gaze reminded her of the glances of the ghosts: cold and hateful.

They drew close to the keep, and there another gate once stood. Now it lay on the courtyard floor, destroyed and twisted.

The ghostly soldiers, still silent, raised their hands in a salute. From the shadows of the gate more of them emerged, but these were different. They were taller men, and their gazes were even fiercer. Their armor gleamed like moonlight, and death charged the air.

One warrior stood in their midst, and Shar knew him for what he was. He was their leader. He was their general, and he was a man like Asana. He walked with grace and purpose. He was calm as a summer's day, yet that did not hide the deadly power within him. He was the storm that could wreak havoc from a blue sky, and she felt fear stab through her.

The general looked at her, and his eyes were piercing as driven nails.

"Why do you disturb our well-earned rest?" he asked.

Shar felt that coldness overcome her that often did at times of peril. Her fear faded away.

"Do you know who I am?"

"I know. Tell me why I should not order you killed? For the swords of my dead soldiers thirst for your blood."

23. Hail, Emperor!

Shar was not afraid. It might be that ghosts could kill, and she must assume the general meant what he said, for he did not look the sort of man to make hollow threats.

But it did not matter. That coldness that enveloped her in times of peril was all about her now, and within her. She looked at him and saw this as a test. She would pass, or she would fail. If destiny were truly on her side in this, her plan would go well. If not, then she could do nothing for her people and life would be a misery.

She stepped closer to the general, careful to move slowly and to show no sign of threat. As if the living could pose one to him, anyway.

For a few heartbeats she looked into the eyes of the dead man. She could make all sorts of arguments to him, but one did not reason with a ghost, still less a general with a thousand soldiers at his command. And her forefather had killed them all.

No. This was not about reasoned arguments. This was about emotion, and from the moment the general had spoken she knew what she must do.

She felt no fear, and she showed none. The eyes of the general studied her, and she knew that in life he had been a hard man and perceptive. Not easily would her ancestor have conquered him.

Still looking him in the eye, she bowed, and then kneeled before him, her arms outspread.

"If it is true," she said in a loud voice, "that the dead can read the hearts of the living, then read mine and judge me. I am not my forefather, yet I may be like him. I did not kill you, yet you might seek revenge in my death. But you know who I am, and what I want. Kill me in revenge if you wish, and I will forgive you. Or let me live, and allow me to do good for my people. You, O general, hold the fate of the Cheng people in your hands."

When she had finished speaking she bowed her head and exposed her neck to a stroke that could kill her. The silence of the night was profound, and the only thing she could hear was that Asana and Kubodin had stepped closer toward her, but then they had ceased to move. They had realized they could not interfere in this, for it was her choice. Or perhaps destiny, if there were such a thing, had stilled them.

The general stepped closer though, and then she heard the ghostly whisper of his sword as he drew it from his bejeweled scabbard. She could not see the blade, but she knew what it would be like. A general's blade was not a battle weapon, but rather thin and graceful like Asana's. And it would be sharp enough to behead her at a stroke.

"Think not that the thirst for revenge lessens in death," the general said, and there was a tightness in his words that spoke of a raging anger controlled by a will of steel.

She did not see the blow coming, nor hear it. Yet the thin blade of the general drew blood from her neck. She did not flinch, even when she realized what had been done.

The steel was cold against her skin, and she felt a trickle of blood run down her neck. She did not move, but she heard Kubodin hiss behind her.

Shar stared at the ground and trusted in fate, or if not that, the freedom of death. She felt the blade withdraw from where it touched her skin, and she could see the steel shod boots of the general before her. They moved slightly, and this time she knew another blow was coming. Against her will, she gasped, but she did not move her head more than an inch.

The blow struck her. Once more it did not kill her, but the blade bit deeper this time. It lingered against her skin, cold as the dead men all around her. Then something strange happened.

With a clatter, the sword hit the ground and then lay still. Before her, the general knelt himself, even as she had done for him.

"Hail the emperor!" the general cried, and all around a thousand ghostly voices answered him.

"We hail the emperor!"

"Rise," the general commanded her. She did so smoothly, and now looked down on him for he did not move.

"You will do great things, if you live," the dead man said. "But I give you this warning. Beware the shamans, for they love you not, and their power is great."

"Yet still I will defy them."

"It may be so, for he who became the emperor in my time defied them also. Yet still they murdered him."

"It is not said at the end though," Shar told him, "that the emperor regretted fighting. Even as he lay dying, he struggled against them."

"It is so. But heed my warning. Trust them not. And if you cannot see them or what they have done, trust them even less, for that is when they are at their most dangerous."

They were wise words, and Shar knew it. But she could do nothing against the dangers she could not see.

Even as she began to form an answer to the general, she saw his ghostly form fade away like mist caught in a breeze. She looked around, and his army was gone also. There was only Asana and Kubodin, staring at her.

181

Shar felt a stinging sensation on both sides of her neck, but when she put her hands to the wounds there was no blood.

Asana looked intently at her skin, and she knew that he had seen blood even as she had felt it, but when he spoke it was not about that.

"You have courage, Shar."

24. The Great Emperor

Shar led her companions into the inner keep of the fortress.

It was darker here, but the ghosts were gone. There was nothing to fear now that they had left. Except the trap of the shamans, if there were one.

Behind her, she heard Kubodin whisper a question to Asana.

"What do you think happened to the ghosts?"

"Gone," the swordmaster replied.

"Yes, but forever? Do they still haunt this place? Or have they found peace at last?"

Shar could not quite hear what answer Asana gave. Whatever it was, it had a chance of being right. She did not think anyone could know, except perhaps her grandmother. Shulu knew these things, and much dark law besides. But if by giving those long-dead soldiers their chance at revenge she had freed them from whatever bound them to the place they had died, she would be glad. Even if her quest failed here, she had done some good in the world.

The light of the torches was fitful, and they found new timber to make more. Whatever roof there had once been, it was now gone. At least in this area. What remained of the rafters littered the floor. As did the bones of the ancient battle. They were as dust though, for she had by ill chance stepped on some. She did not wish to do that, but in places the floor was so thick with them that it was impossible to avoid. The fighting had been fierce.

She soon saw why. There was a stairway here leading to some smaller and more secure room farther to the back of the keep and above.

The stairs were of stone. They too were littered with the ancient remnants of battle, and under the light of the torches she could see the steps were stained with ancient blood. She did not wish to tread them, but she must.

"This way," she said, and began to ascend.

"We haven't explored all of this level," Kubodin replied.

"I know. But I don't think the shamans would have hidden the swords down here."

She was not sure what made her say that. The swords could be anywhere, yet she did feel something from up above pulling at her. Maybe it was just her imagination. Or maybe it was some sense of her destiny guiding her as it had done with the general.

She walked up the stairs, moving slowly. For the first time she drew her sword, for she did not know what was up there and could see little. At one point, she rested her other hand against a wooden balustrade, but it turned to dust at her touch.

At the top of the stairs was a smaller room, but still quite large. It led to a tower of some sort, and there was another staircase. This she followed, drawn upwards like a plant seeking sunlight. She knew that whatever awaited her was at the top of this tower.

For whatever reason, this part of the keep was in much better repair than the rest. Both ceilings and floors remained sturdy, and even the handrails seemed solid, but she rested no weight against them.

They ascended five levels, and at last came to the highest one. It was still a fair-sized room, some fifty feet in diameter, and all their torches only lit it partly.

Shar crept ahead. She wedged her torch in a crevice in the floor, and the others did likewise. No word was spoken, but they all wanted their hands free in order to better wield their weapons.

Without doubt, the last stand of the ancient defenders of the fortress had taken place here. Armor and bones lay thick on the floor, and the smell of decay was still detectable all these years later.

There had been a fire here too. It had burned the floor away to their left, but for some reason had been put out. Perhaps the emperor had thought to use the fortress for himself one day.

"Over there," Asana said softly.

Shar knew what he meant. There was something catching the light against the far wall, and it was higher than ground level. It was not some armor of a dead soldier.

She moved closer. Asana and Kubodin fanned out to her left and right. Outside the fortress a wind had begun blowing, and it must have been strong. It moaned now inside the chamber, finding entry through small gaps in the roof and exiting down the fire-ruined floor now behind them. She felt the touch of that air on her face, and she did not like it. It reminded her of the ghosts.

It did not take long to see what gleamed in the light. It was a door, but this one was of bronze. Carefully, Shar tried to push it open, but it did not move and there was no handle. Yet it must be a door, for there was nothing else up here in this chamber, and she knew her destiny lay on the other side. But she could not budge it.

Asana drew close and he leaned against it, pressing with all his strength. Nothing happened, but from an inner pocket the little statue of Shulu Gan tumbled out and clattered loudly against the floor. He bent down to pick it up, but he stayed there, looking at the floor itself where the door joined it.

"There seems to be some mechanism here," he whispered.

A moment later there was a sudden clink, and Shar leaped back with her sword to the ready. But all that happened was that a slow groan filled the air as something moved that had not done so for a long time. The door opened, not inward or outward, but sliding sideways into a recess.

Beyond, a room was revealed. They went inside, Shar at the front. The floor here was clean, and the timber was overlaid with terracotta tiles in zigzag patterns. The walls were hung with tapestries, long since rotting, but here and there scenes of battling armies, forests and waterfalls remained. The roof glittered. It was a dome of gold or brass. Shar could not tell which.

But none of these things drew her gaze. In the center of the room upon a dais stood a statue, and her attention was on that and nothing else.

She heard Asana gasp. "It is the likeness of the emperor."

Shar had never seen an image of him, but Asana was a learned man. He would have seen it in books that never made it to the fen, and she believed him. She studied the image carefully.

The man she looked at was tall for a Cheng, and his bright gaze was fierce and intelligent. Those eyes were violet, and they caught the dim light of the torches from the outer room. His hair was jet black, held back in a tight bun. He had a wispy but long mustache, and a pointed beard. In this, there were touches of gray and she believed that this really was the likeness of her great ancestor, and probably not long before his death.

The robes were carved beautifully. They were of many-colored silks, and they fell away from his shoulders just as clothes would have in real life. Yet he wore not just clothes but also an armored vest. It was of rectangular sheets of metal, gold plated, and riveted together. It was only the vest though. The rest of it, including the helm, was missing. These items, along with two scabbards, lay on a low table to his side.

What was not missing though were his swords. The fabled twin swords were in his grip, and the blades gleamed as legend told with two slightly different colors. One represented the dusk, and the other dawn. The pommel stone of each was amethyst, and they matched his eyes.

Shar gazed at those swords in awe. They were not a part of the statue. They were *real*. They were the twin swords at last that many had sought but none, until now, had found. It was they that had called to her ever since she had entered the fortress.

They all stepped closer, but Shar paused again. The swords were within reach now. She could almost feel them in her hands, but something disturbed her.

"This is too easy," she said.

The others did not reply, but they made no move to encourage her. They felt it too.

Shar moved around the statue, circling it twice. She could see nothing wrong. Asana and Kubodin studied it closely, but they merely shook their heads. They could find nothing wrong either.

Standing before it again, Shar looked once more into those violet eyes. Even as she did so, a glimmer of moonlight struck them through a window and they gleamed. The gaze that looked back at her was so lifelike that she involuntarily stepped back, but then she steadied herself.

187

"I can sense no trap," she said.

"Nor I," Kubodin replied.

"What about you, Asana?" she asked.

"I sense nothing either. But the seer warned of one, and his words have proved true in all respects."

Shar had not forgotten. "Yet what am I to do? Stand and wait here in doubt for all eternity?"

Her companions sensed her impatience. But they did not encourage her to take the blades. That must be her choice, and hers alone. They had her back though. No matter what happened, they would stand with her. They had proved that already, and she felt the bond that had grown between them. She wanted to take the swords, but she would not do so if she put them at risk. Yet what risk was there?

None that she could see.

Long moments she stood there, undecided. The shaft of moonlight through the window came and went, and the eyes of the emperor glimmered like starlight. Or the points of spears.

There was nothing left to do though except to take the swords. It was that, or turn around and leave. The thought of doing so spurred her to action, and she slowly reached out her hands toward the blades.

"One more thing," Asana said. "I do not doubt who you are. I believe, for Shulu Gan told me so. Yet I must remind you of this. According to legend, it is death for any but the heir of the emperor to touch those swords."

Shar paused in mid reach. She knew that. She had heard it all her life. No child among the Cheng had not listened to the story a hundred times. Likewise, she had been told who she was since she was old enough to be trusted with the truth. But all that she knew, and all that Asana knew, came from the same source. It all stemmed from Shulu Gan. Yet what if she was not Shulu? Or what if it was all a lie?

It was a thought that had occurred to her before, and she had always dismissed it. The difference now though was that her very life depended on it being true.

25. A Beacon of War

Shar still hesitated. She believed all that her grandmother had told her, and she was willing to risk her life on the bond of trust between them. But another thought occurred to her.

"It *is* a trap," she said.

"What have you seen?" Asana asked.

"Nothing. Yet why would the shamans build a statue of their enemy? They would not honor him like that."

"You're right," Asana answered immediately.

"I know it. I feel it. I think there is magic in the statue and it will flare to life when I touch it."

Kubodin lifted his axe a little higher. "That makes sense to me. Does it change anything, though?"

"Nothing at all. Not for me. I'll take the risk for my people, but you need not. You should leave the fortress. Or at the very least this room."

"We're not going anywhere," Kubodin told her.

"And they are our people also," Asana added.

Shar felt proud to have such true friends, but all she could say in return was to give a warning.

"Then prepare yourselves, for I'm done hesitating."

She wished she could have told them how she felt about them, but just like that coldness settled over her in times of peril she was not good at showing her feelings. She did not like that about herself, and wished she could be better. Maybe one day she would be.

She stepped a little closer to the statue, and she raised her sword in a defensive position. The blade offered no protection against magic, but she felt better doing so.

Then she stepped to the side. It was foolish, but she mistrusted the pose of the statue. It was crafted so lifelike and looked as though it might attack. She felt better coming in from the side with her blade up to protect her just as she would have approached a real opponent.

There was nothing to do now but keep going, and she slowly reached out to touch one of the hilts. At that first contact a thrill ran through her. It speared through her fingertips and into her heart, and she knew these were the real swords and that her fate was attached to them.

Yet even as that thrill ran through her, the violet eyes of the statue blinked and turned crimson. By some dark magic the metal from which it was made came to life. With a groan, the likeness of the emperor struck at her, and had her own sword not been up she would have been killed.

Shar reeled backward under the force of that blow, and she fell sprawling to the floor. A moment later, she was up again and Asana and Kubodin spread out around her, weapons at the ready.

"This is my test to pass or fail," she said. "Stay back."

Her friends moved reluctantly out of the way. The statue stalked toward her, and Shar wondered at what sort of magic could give life to metal. It was as real as a person now, but that might be its weakness. If the magic could make it soft enough to move, then could not her blade cut it like flesh?

The statue shuffled forward, the twin swords swirling in a pattern before it. Then it lunged, sending one blade at Shar's stomach and another at her head. The thing moved with lightning speed, and few would have survived that attack.

But Shar did. She had trained all her life, pushed by her grandmother and taught in ways that few other warriors ever were. Leaning back and edging a little to the side, she avoided the blows and launched her own strike. It was a slash toward her opponent's neck, and the statue jumped back to avoid it.

The two combatants circled each other warily, but Shar had learned something. This enemy of dark sorcery, made of metal as it was, was vulnerable to injury as she had thought. Otherwise, it would have had no need to evade her blow.

As they circled, that familiar sense of coldness settled deep into Shar. Gone was all emotion, and life and death were one to her. All that held her attention was the play of blades.

The statue attacked again, the twin swords a whirl of flashing steel and deadly intent. Shar wondered if somehow the skill of the emperor had been captured in the magic, for this opponent was greater even than the Ahat she had fought.

She fell back under the onslaught, if slowly. The statue was like her, void of all emotion, and she did not doubt that if it killed her it would move back to its original position, turn back into metal and remain still for centuries, or eternity, waiting for another to touch it.

But there would be no other heir. So far as she knew, she was the last to walk the earth, or at least her grandmother had said so. And if she died, no more descendants of the emperor's blood would ever come again.

Something ruffled the coldness that gripped her, and a stroke of the enemy nearly gutted her, but then the coldness returned and she danced to the side, striking at the statue's head.

There was a dull thud as the tip of her blade bit home. The creature of magic retreated, a slight gash marking its head, but there was no blood.

She expected a counterattack of fury, as another human would have done. Or a retreat in fear, but neither occurred. The statue merely circled again, calculating its next attack with precision.

Shar met it when it came, her sword deflecting her opponent's even as she pivoted to the side. This was her way of negating the second blade of the enemy, and it had worked well so far. Yet this time the creature anticipated her move and spun swift as thought, bringing the second blade back into the fight again.

There was a crack of blade against blade and the whoosh of the second one near her face, but Shar managed to avoid death and skip back to create space again, or so she thought. But the creature pursued her relentlessly now, both swords swirling in deadly attacks.

The dark thought of defeat began to shadow Shar's mind. She could not beat this thing. Already she was beginning to tire, but the statue did not. Before long, she would make a mistake and it would be all over.

Shar reeled to the side, and then danced back and forward to the other side. She was not fast enough to throw her opponent's balance off, but her move did end its pursuit. The two combatants circled again, and Shar thought faster than she ever had before. She would have few chances left.

It became obvious to her that there was only one thing to do. The magic of the creature understood battle, but how well did it understand human behavior and stratagems? The shade-warriors that her grandmother conjured for her to fight had not.

She took a deep breath, and withdrew one of her knives. She saw the violet eyes of her enemy focus on that new threat, and they watched her as she lobbed the weapon high into the air. But the moment the knife went above its head, the eyes switched back to Shar. It saw no danger in the knife, and dismissed it.

The knife reached the top of its arc, and there it slowed momentarily before plummeting to earth again. It struck a glancing blow to the statue's right shoulder on the way down, and the thing turned in that direction, swords flashing against a foe that was not there.

Shar lunged. This would be her only opportunity, and she had to make the most of it. Her weight shifted to the front foot, and she put all the strength of her arm and the momentum of her body behind it. If it failed, she would be badly exposed to a counterattack.

It did not fail. The point of her sword struck the statue, and pierced the malleable metal. It drove in deeper, until it came out the creature's back, and Shar kept pushing and driving upward at the same time.

The statue made no sound, but it thrashed in the death throes of its magic. The twin swords clattered to the floor, and the statue pulled Shar's own sword from her grip as it stumbled. Then suddenly as it had come to life it died and turned to hard, immoveable metal once more, her sword fixed forever through it.

Shar moved swiftly to gather up the twin swords. She had no time to marvel at the feel of them in her hands for a crimson vapor erupted from the mouth of the statue, and it rose high toward the domed ceiling. It ignited in a sudden flash and with a thunderous boom, causing a pillar of flame to course upward and smash into the ceiling. Pressure built for a moment, and then the roof lifted and slid a little sideways as though it weighed no more than paper.

"The magic that made the statue is dying!" Kubodin cried.

Shar joined the other two and together they backed away. She was terrified of the force of nature being unleashed here, but at the same time she could not take her eyes off it.

There was a flash of pain in her hands though, and she sensed the magic of the twin swords come to life. It ran up through her arms and into her head, and there was a sharp pain in her eyes. Then it was gone.

Shar staggered, then quickly righted herself. Kubodin was there as well, an arm around her shoulder to steady her.

Asana glanced at her, and saw that she was not hurt. He turned to look at the statue again, but then his head swung back to her, and he stared at her face.

"Your eyes!"

Shar could not see what he saw, but she knew. All her life she had been told what to expect at this moment. The spell that disguised her, the magic that darkened her eyes and protected her from being murdered by any shaman who saw her, would be released when she gripped the twin swords and the magic that was in them dispelled it.

Asana went on one knee. "Hail, emperor-to-be!" he shouted above the tumult.

Kubodin eyed her, and even he, irreverent as he was, looked strangely solemn. He also went on bended knee.

"Hail, emperor-that-was-foretold!"

Shar bent her head to them, and then she smiled feeling as though a thousand suns warmed her heart with joy.

"Perhaps I shall be emperor, but that road is a long one to journey. For now, we must escape!"

What reply either one of them would have given, Shar never heard. At that moment another voice rang out, and it was deep and solemn, cold as metal but thrumming like a bell.

Hail, child of the emperor! And hail to thee, my brother!

Shar nearly dropped the swords, for the voice reverberated from the blades themselves. She stood, struck mute by surprise, and into the silence another voice gave answer.

195

Hail, brother of the void! Long it has been since last we met, and the days have been dull.

Shar began to tremble, for that second voice rang out from Kubodin's axe.

Those days are done, the swords replied. *Rejoice! For the chaos ahead will bring bloodshed across the land to slake even the thirst of our kind.*

The weapons spoke no more, and silence fell. Yet the crimson flame of the statue flashed and surged. The domed roof of the room blew completely away now, tumbling in ruin and a clatter of stone as it struck the wall of the keep. But the roaring crimson flame did not stop. Rather it leaped like a fountain into the nighttime sky.

Out of the crimson flame a form appeared, swirling and twisting into shape. It was the image of a shaman, stern and authoritative. It stepped from the fire into the room and addressed Shar.

"Think not that you have succeeded, child of the emperor. You have not, nor ever will. The might of the shamans will crush you, and your fate is sealed. A beacon of war lights up the sky, and the eyes of every shaman for hundreds of miles is drawn to it. We know where you are, and I have now seen you. All the land will hunt for you, and—"

The image of the shaman got no further, for the twin swords in Shar's hand cut the air in gleaming arcs, cutting it to pieces. Whatever magic sustained it was sundered, and wherever the true body of the shaman was that magic would have come flooding back to it, bringing pain and maybe even death. Such at least was the lore that Shulu had taught Shar, and she believed it. She believed it all, now.

Kubodin laughed with joy. "That put him in his place!"

Asana was more serious. "Time to go. Whatever you think of shamans, I don't think he was lying. We must leave here swiftly and hide, for soon this place will be overrun with enemies."

They raced away then, Shar sparing only enough time to dart toward the statue and gather up the two scabbards that lay on the table near it. But she had no time to belt them, nor would she have sheathed the swords if she could. There could be enemies already seeking her in the fortress, for surely there must be shamans close by.

"What *were* those voices?" Shar asked as they hastened ahead.

Kubodin knew exactly what she meant, and he grinned as he answered. "Big magic. Bad magic, but good for us. I've been told, and I believe it, that Shulu Gan made weapons at the height of her powers. And in the greatest of them she trapped a demon inside the blades. That's where they get their magic from. That's why they can't be destroyed."

Shar shuddered as she ran. She did not like that, and she foresaw problems. All magic had consequences, and they could be dire here. Whatever problems arose though, they would be for another day.

When they at last left the killing tunnel inside the fortress wall and came to the outside through the ruined gateway, dawn was sweeping over the land. Yet the pillar of fire lit the sky crimson behind them. Half the land must be seeing it and wondering what it was. Except for the shamans.

Outside the gate there also waited those other questers who had followed them. They had not gone in the fortress, but they could still be a danger.

Shar decided to deal with this swiftly. She strode toward them, the twin swords in her hands and the amethyst pommel stones gleaming, but it was to her eyes that they pointed and exclaimed.

"By these swords, you know who I am. These eyes confirm it. Do you acknowledge me?"

Shar was not sure what to expect. If these were bad men, they might try to take the swords for themselves and she would be forced to kill them.

But they made no hostile move. Instead, once that initial shock of seeing her was over, some bowed deeply while others knelt.

"You are the emperor's heir!" one said.

"I am. And I have a task for you. Being heir is nothing unless I live to unite the tribes. Will you help me? *Dare* you help me? For all the might of the shamans will be against us."

Thus ends *Swords of Empire*. The Shaman's Sword series continues in book two, *Swords of Wizardry*, where Shar must try to evade the dark power of the enemy while she struggles to forge an empire out of a mass of tribes divided by lies, mistrust and the intrigues of the shamans…

SWORDS OF WIZARDRY

BOOK TWO OF THE SHAMAN'S SWORD SERIES

COMING SOON!

Amazon lists millions of titles, and I'm glad you discovered this one. But if you'd like to know when I release a new book, instead of leaving it to chance, sign up for my new release list. I'll send you an email on publication.

Yes please! – Go to www.homeofhighfantasy.com and sign up.

No thanks – I'll take my chances.

Dedication

There's a growing movement in fantasy literature. Its name is noblebright, and it's the opposite of grimdark.

Noblebright celebrates the virtues of heroism. It's an old-fashioned thing, as old as the first story ever told around a smoky campfire beneath ancient stars. It's storytelling that highlights courage and loyalty and hope for the spirit of humanity. It recognizes the dark, the dark in us all, and the dark in the villains of its stories. It recognizes death, and treachery and betrayal. But it dwells on none of these things.

I dedicate this book, such as it is, to that which is noblebright. And I thank the authors before me who held the torch high so that I could see the path: J.R.R. Tolkien, C.S. Lewis, Terry Brooks, Susan Cooper, Roger Taylor and many others. I salute you.

And, for a time, I too shall hold the torch high.

Appendix: Encyclopedic Glossary

Note: The history of the Cheng Empire is obscure, for the shamans hid much of it. Yet the truth was recorded in many places and passed down in family histories, in secret societies and especially among warrior culture. This glossary draws on much of that 'secret' history, and each book in this series is individualized to reflect the personal accounts that have come down through the dark tracts of time to the main actors within each book's pages. Additionally, there is often historical material provided in its entries for people, artifacts and events that are not included in the main text.

Many races dwell in Alithoras. All have their own language, and though sometimes related to one another the changes sparked by migration, isolation and various influences often render these tongues unintelligible to each other.

The ascendancy of Halathrin culture across the land, who are sometimes called elves, combined with their widespread efforts to secure and maintain allies against various evil incursions, has made their language the primary means of communication between diverse peoples. This was especially so during the Shadowed Wars, but has persisted through the centuries afterward.

This glossary contains a range of names and terms. Some are of Halathrin origin, and their meaning is provided.

The Cheng culture is also revered by its people, and many names are given in their tongue. It is important to remember that the empire was vast though, and there is no one Cheng language but rather a multitude of dialects. Perfect consistency of spelling and meaning is therefore not to be looked for.

List of abbreviations:

Cam. Camar

Chg. Cheng

Comb. Combined

Cor. Corrupted form

Hal. Halathrin

Prn. Pronounced

Ahat: *Chg.* "Hawk in the night." A special kind of assassin. Used by the shamans in particular, but open for hire to anybody who can afford their fee. It is said that the shamans subverted an entire tribe in the distant past, and that every member of the community, from the children to the elderly, train to hone their craft at killing and nothing else. They grow no crops, raise no livestock nor pursue any trade save the bringing of death. The fees of their assignments pay for all their needs. This is legend only, for no such community has ever been found. But the lands of the Cheng are wide and such a community, if it exists, would be hidden and guarded.

Alithoras: *Hal.* "Silver land." The Halathrin name for the continent they settled after leaving their own homeland. Refers to the extensive river and lake systems they found and their wonder at the beauty of the land.

Argash: *Chg.* "The clamor of war." A warrior of the Fen Wolf Tribe, and leader of one band of the leng-fah. His great-grandfather was once chief of the clan.

Asana: *Chg.* "Gift of light." Rumored to be the greatest swordmaster in the history of the Cheng people. His father was a Duthenor tribesman from outside the bounds of the old Cheng Empire.

Chatchek Fortress: *Chg.* "Hollow mountain." An ancient fortress once conquered by Chen Fei. It predates the Cheng Empire however, having been constructed two thousand years prior to that time. It is said it was established to protect a trade route where gold was mined and transported to the surrounding lands.

Chen Fei: *Chg.* "Graceful swan." Swans are considered birds of wisdom and elegance in Cheng culture. It is said that one flew overhead at the time of Chen's birth, and his mother named him for it. He rose from poverty to become emperor of his people, and he was loved by many but despised by some. He was warrior, general, husband, father, poet, philosopher, painter, but most of all he was enemy to the machinations of the shamans who tried to secretly govern all aspects of the people.

Cheng: *Chg.* "Warrior." The overall name of the various related tribes united by Chen Fei. It was a word for warrior in his dialect, later adopted for his growing army and last of all for the people of his nation. His empire disintegrated after his assassination, but much of the culture he fostered endured.

Cheng Empire: A vast array of realms formerly governed by kings and united, briefly, under Chen Fei. One of the largest empires ever to rise in Alithoras.

Dar shun: *Chg.* "The points that vibrate." The art of using the pressure points of the human body to heal, harm or kill. A secret skill passed down in elite warrior and healer societies. Its knowledge and workings are revered, and only handed down to students of high moral character. Except for the Ahat. But even among them it is taught to few.

Eagle Claw Mountains: A mountain range toward the south of the Cheng Empire. It is said the people who later became the Cheng lived here first and over centuries moved out to populate the surrounding lands. Others believe that these people were blue-eyed, and intermixed with various other races as they came down off the mountains to trade and make war.

Elves: See Halathrin.

Elù-haraken: *Hal.* "The shadowed wars." Long ago battles in a time that is become myth to the Cheng tribes.

Fen Wolf Tribe: A tribe that live in Tsarin Fen. Once, they and the neighboring Soaring Eagle Tribe were one people and part of a kingdom. It is also told that Chen Fei was born in that realm.

Fields of Rah: Rah signifies "ocean of the sky" in many Cheng dialects. It is a country of vast grasslands but at its center is Nagrak City, which of old was the capital of the empire. It was in this city that the emperor was assassinated.

Gan: *Chg.* "They who have attained." It is an honorary title added to a person's name after they have acquired great skill. It can be applied to warriors, shamans, sculptors, weavers or any particular expertise. It is reserved for the greatest of the best.

Ghirlock: *Chg.* "The goat that flies." A bird of the snipe species. Associated with the supernatural and the elemental gods of the Cheng. Its sound in flight is like the bleat of a goat.

Go Shan: *Chg.* "Daughter of wisdom." An epithet of Shulu Gan.

Halath: *Hal.* King of the Halathrin. He died long ago. He led his people on their exodus to Alithoras, and was revered and loved as a great ruler.

Halathrin: *Hal.* "People of Halath." A race of elves named after an honored lord who led an exodus of his people to the land of Alithoras in pursuit of justice, having sworn to defeat a great evil. They are human, though of fairer form, greater skill and higher culture. They possess a unity of body, mind and spirit that enables insight and endurance beyond the native races of Alithoras. Said to be immortal, but killed in great numbers during their conflicts in ancient times with the evil they sought to destroy. Those conflicts are collectively known as the Shadowed Wars.

Halls of Lore: Essentially, a library within the stronghold of the lòhrens in northern Alithoras. It serves as a repository for the known history of humanity and the wisdom of the ages.

Harakness: *Chg.* "The tears of the earth." The Cheng god of water.

Heart of the Hurricane: The shaman's term for the state of mind warriors call Stillness in the Storm. See that term for further information.

Kubodin: *Chg.* Etymology unknown. A wild warrior from the Wahlum Hills. Simple appearing, but far more than he seems. Asana's manservant and friend.

Leng-fah: *Chg.* "Wolf skills." An organization of warrior scouts who patrol the borders of Tsarin Fen to protect its people from hostile incursions by other tribes. They take their name from the swamp wolf, a creature of great stealth and cunning. This is the totem animal of the Fen Wolf tribe.

Lòhren: *Hal. Prn.* Ler-ren. "Knowledge giver – a counselor." Other terms used by various nations include sage, wizard, and druid.

Magic: Mystic power.

Malach Gan: *Chg.* "Grinding ice – the front edge of a mountain glacier." A lòhren of Cheng descent. Rumored to be related to Asana. Though he is proficient in the arts of magic, he is not a shaman and the Cheng people call him a sage by way of distinction.

Nadral: *Chg.* "Dew-on-the-grass." An old warrior of the Nagrak Tribe.

Nahaz: *Chg.* "White fire." A spirit fermented from mare's milk. Originated in the Nagrak Tribe, but traded throughout the tribes. Said to possess recuperative powers, and used in many rituals.

Nagrak: *Chg.* "Those who follow the herds." A Cheng tribe that dwell on the Fields of Rah. Traditionally they lived a nomadic lifestyle, traveling in the wake of herds of wild cattle that provided all their needs. But an element of their tribe, and some contend this was another tribe in origin that they conquered, are great builders and live in a city.

Nagrak City: A city at the heart of the Fields of Rah. Once the capital of the Cheng Empire.

Nagrak gul sak viran: "Peace of the Nagrak earth and sky upon you." A ritual Nagrak greeting.

Nagrak gul sak yohan: "Peace of the Nagrak earth and sky upon us all." A ritual Nagrak response to a greeting.

Nazram: *Chg.* "The wheat grains that are prized after the chaff is excluded." An elite warrior organization that is in service to the shamans. For the most part, they are selected from those who quest for the twin swords each triseptium, though there are exceptions to this.

Nefu: *Chg.* "Shadows on the desert." An assassin.

Nuhar: *Chg.* "The hunted one." A term of various uses. Famed, however, as the description the Ahat use for a designated assassination mark.

Olekhai: *Chg.* "The falcon that plummets." A famous and often used name in the old world before, and during, the

Cheng Empire. Never used since the assassination of the emperor, however. The most prominent bearer of the name during the days of the emperor was the chief of his council of wise men. He was, essentially, prime minister of the emperor's government. But he betrayed his lord and his people. Shulu Gan spared his life, but only so as to punish him with a terrible curse.

Quest of Swords: Occurs every triseptium to mark the three times seven years the shamans lived in exile during the emperor's life. The best warriors of each clan seek the twin swords of the emperor. Used by the shamans as a means of finding the most skilled warriors in the land and recruiting them to their service.

Shade-warriors: Warriors of illusion summoned by magic for the purposes of sparring during warrior training sessions. Although illusionary, they appear real to the other combatant, even down to the jarring of sword against sword. Very few shamans possess the skill to create them.

Shadowed Wars: See Elù-haraken.

Shapechanger: Prominent figures in Cheng legend and history. They are beings able to take any form, and are renowned for being mischievous. Other stories, or histories, claim they are creatures of evil in servitude to the shamans.

Shaman: The religious leaders of the Cheng people. They are sorcerers, and though the empire is fragmented they work as one across the lands to serve their own united purpose. Their spiritual home is Three Moon Mountain, but few save shamans have ever been there.

Shar: *Chg.* "White stone – the peak of a mountain." A young woman of the Fen Wolf tribe. Claimed by Shulu Gan to be the descendent of Chen Fei.

Shulu Gan: *Chg.* The first element signifies "magpie." A name given to the then leader of the shamans for her hair was black, save for a streak of white that ran through it.

Soaring Eagle Tribe: A tribe that borders the Fen Wolf Clan. At one time, one with them, but now, as is the situation with most tribes, hostilities are common. The eagle is their totem, for the birds are plentiful in the mountain lands to the south and often soar far from their preferred habitat over the tribe's grasslands.

Stillness in the Storm: The state of mind a true warrior seeks in battle. Neither angry nor scared, neither hopeful nor worried. When emotion is banished from the mind, the body is free to express the skill acquired through long years of training. Sometimes also called Calmness in the Storm or the Heart of the Hurricane.

Taga Nashu: *Chg.* "The Grandmother who does not die." One of the many epithets of Shulu Gan, greatest of the shamans but cast from their order.

Tarok: *Chg.* "The warrior who endures." A warrior of the Soaring Eagle Tribe. Was once a nazram, but forsook his duties and returned to the land of his birth. It is said he did this because he came to despise the leadership of the nazram organization.

Three Moon Mountain: A mountain in the Eagle Claw range. Famed as the home of the shamans. None know what the three moons reference relates to except, perhaps, the shamans.

Triseptium: A period of three times seven years. It signifies the exiles of the shamans during the life of the emperor. Declared by the shamans as a cultural treasure, and celebrated by them. Less so by the tribes, but the shamans encourage it. Much more popular now than in past ages.

Tsarin Fen: *Chg.* Tsarin, which signifies mountain cat, was a general under Chen Fei. It is said he retired to the swamp after the death of his leader. At one time, many regions and villages were named after generals, but the shamans changed the names and did all they could to make people forget the old ones. In their view, all who served the emperor were criminals and their achievements were not to be celebrated. Tsarin Fen is one of the few such names that still survive.

Wahlum Hills: *Chg. Comb. Hal.* "Mist-shrouded highlands." Hills to the north-west of the old Cheng empire, and home to Kubodin.

Wizard: See lòhren.

About the author

I'm a man born in the wrong era. My heart yearns for faraway places and even further afield times. Tolkien had me at the beginning of *The Hobbit* when he said, ". . . one morning long ago in the quiet of the world . . ."

Sometimes I imagine myself in a Viking mead-hall. The long winter night presses in, but the shimmering embers of a log in the hearth hold back both cold and dark. The chieftain calls for a story, and I take a sip from my drinking horn and stand up . . .

Or maybe the desert stars shine bright and clear, obscured occasionally by wisps of smoke from burning camel dung. A dry gust of wind marches sand grains across our lonely campsite, and the wayfarers about me stir restlessly. I sip cool water and begin to speak.

I'm a storyteller. A man to paint a picture by the slow music of words. I like to bring faraway places and times to life, to make hearts yearn for something they can never have, unless for a passing moment.

Printed in Great Britain
by Amazon